Fifty Hues Of Hairy Legs And Morning Breath

By Camille R Harding

Fifty Hues of Hairy Legs and Morning Breath

First published in 2013 by
New Dawn Publishers Ltd
292 Rochfords Gardens
Slough, Berkshire SL2 5XW

www.newdawnpublishersltd.co.uk

newdawnpublishersltd@gmail.com

ISBN 9781-908462-05-3

ABOUT THE AUTHOR

Camille R Harding was born and raised in London, but she has also lived in Greece and Australia. She currently resides with her husband in South-East London.

Camille has a degree in communication and cultural studies and a PGCE in English. This is Camille's first work of fiction, having previously written reviews and articles for local newspapers and websites.

When Camille is not writing, she is also the lead singer of covers band *The Daredevils*.

DEDICATION

For my wonderful husband Rob, my mum Carol
Smith and my best friend Katy Ward- the three most
important and funniest people in my life.

Chapter 1 - The Interview

My name is Annabella Stevens. I'm twenty one and an English Literature student. I have an annoying inner goddess (you're probably wondering what that is; well to tell you the truth I haven't got a clue either, but I've heard that including one in a book or three can make you a bloody fortune) and an equally annoying subconscious who will pop up at any given opportunity. I'm still a virgin, which I'm well aware is rather unbelievable since all students seem to do these days is get drunk and shag each other.

I share a flat with my friend Kayleigh who I think is far prettier, cleverer and exciting than me. Well let's be honest Annabella she is. Oh dear she speaks so soon; reader- meet my subconscious, subconscious- meet the reader and please try not to irritate him/her too much.

I'm supposed to be intelligent and articulate, but I'm really rather stupid and naïve and how I manage to get a degree at the end of all of this is beyond belief to be quite honest.

Anyway, Kayleigh was supposed to be interviewing a well-known millionaire today (as you do when you're a university nobody) called Christopher Green for the student newspaper, but she has a cold (personally I think she's putting it on so that she can stay at home and watch Hollyoaks) so I've agreed to do it.

My journey to Mr Green's office is a friggin nightmare. First on the list of things to piss me off, is the sweaty cyclist with fat arse who cycles in the middle of my lane; he is not wearing a helmet and he has Bill Bailey hair. I want to ram the bonnet of my car into his giant derriere (men with lady bums = just plain wrong) then take a pair of shears to his barnet. Fat arse cyclist is followed by temporary traffic lights and road works, then by a bird shitting on my windscreen; there's a splat of greenish white goo so large that I'm actually convinced it came from a Pterodactyl. I then have to find a parking space, which takes almost the same amount of time as it did to drive here, and of course, this being England, it starts to rain which means I get wet feet and a frizz head walking from my car to the office.

To top it all off, a workman drilling part of the pavement tells me to 'Cheer up love, might never happen'. I have to fight the urge to tell him that my whole family were butchered to death by an axe wielding maniac, which is why I'm a little sad today. Instead I mutter 'Oh fuck off,' and imagine drilling a hole through his forehead. My inner goddess simply giggles as she can see his builder's bum and it is hairy. I would so much rather be at home eating a Kit Kat Chunky in my dressing gown.

The building is a massive twenty storey office block; if the lift is out of order, there is no bloody way I'm walking up the stairs. Of course the lift won't be out of order stupid, this is a swanky Chelsea building, not a council estate in Hackney, sneers my subconscious.

I'm greeted in the lobby by an attractive, well-dressed blonde; I eye the parting of her hair to see if she's a natural as her eyebrows look suspiciously dark.

"I'm here to see Mr Green," I tell her. "Annabella Stevens for Kayleigh Watson."

She disappears for a few moments, then returns with a lanyard and plastic card that says 'visitor' on it. I chuckle to myself as I contemplate whether I'll be one of those twats who wears their lanyard on the train on their way home, like all those office dickheads who wear their name badges in the high street during their lunch break to make themselves feel important. She hands me the lanyard and card and asks me to sign in. Then she leads me to the lifts and tells me to go to the twentieth floor. The lift plays some naff piped music and says good morning to me. I say good morning back and then giggle at my own joke, loser, coughs my subconscious. I disagree and think I am side-splitting. When I exit the lift I am greeted by another attractive blonde, definitely not a natural and with slight bingo-wings, she's obviously getting on a bit.

"Good morning Miss Stevens, Mr Green will just be a few minutes, can I get you something to drink- tea, coffee, water?"

Not impressed with the boring selection of drinks- I was thinking more along the lines of Snake Bite & Black, Magners or a Jaeger bomb. I shake my head and reply.

"No thank you."

After several minutes she tells me that Mr Green is ready to see me and she leads me towards the double doors of his office. I push the doors open and there he is; I stare at him open mouthed, a little bit of dribble escaping from my bottom lip. He is bloody gorgeous! My inner goddess wolf whistles loudly and gyrates her hips; she puts her nipple tassels on and covers herself in chocolate body paint, then struts around to Right Said Fred's 'I'm Too Sexy'. Oh sit down and be quiet will you, that ridiculous body paint makes you look like a dancing turd, my subconscious scolds her. I sense there will be beef between those two. I take in Christopher's physical appearance; tall, bright grey smouldering eyes and unruly dark copper hair. Um. I think you'll find it is ginger actually, mutters my subconscious. I am so busy eyeing him up that when I go to take a step forward into his office, I miss my footing and fall right onto my hands and knees. Well that's the first time you've been on all fours, comes a snigger. I am absolutely mortified and wish I could just disappear.

Fifty Hues of Hairy Legs and Morning Breath

Once I have regained my composure, the interview begins. I find out that Christopher is twenty seven years old and it takes a few minutes for this to sink in. I don't know any twenty seven year old business tycoons; most twenty seven year old men I know are either still living with their mum (who still washes their underpants) whilst trying to pay off their student loan, or renting a shoe box in Clapham with four rugby types and squandering their wages each month on beer, the odd bit of porn and X Box games. I also find out that he is an arrogant control freak who likes to fly in his spare time. Not sure whether he means he takes a lot of LSD and stands on the roof top of buildings whilst tripping out, or has multiple personality disorder thus thinking he is R Kelly.

At one stage during the interview he informs me that he likes to build things; I have a vision of him sitting in his pyjamas building model aeroplanes, whilst his train set chugs around his loft and his telescope sits neatly in its stand- for a moment the sex appeal is gone; goodbye stud, hello trainspotter type nerd. I also find out that he is adopted and he is not gay (although the perfect matching of colours, the elegant yet subtle soft furnishings and feng shui in his office would suggest otherwise).

Anyway the rest of the interview goes something like this; intense stares, raised eyebrows, doe eyed glances, lip biting from me, bottom lip stroking with long (slightly E.T like) fingers from him, feelings of electricity blah-blah-blah. My subconscious is bored and my inner goddess is smoking a fag, flicking her ash into an empty packet of cheese and onion crisps. To cut a long story short, he fancies me (although being stupid and naïve, I don't pick up on this until somewhere near the end of this story) and I fancy him and it is inevitable that we're gonna shag, a lot.

Chapter 2 - Wilko, Photo Shoot and Vomit

It is Saturday and I've just started my shift at Wilkinson. I bloody hate this job; the money is shit and when it is my turn to go on the tills I have to go next to Maureen who can never scan the items in properly because of her acrylic nails. She has a badly dyed perm and smells of Lambert & Butler which she tries to disguise with Impulse body spray. Her skin is like old boot leather, due to her frequent visits to Glam-a-Tan at the end of the high street (and no doubt her numerous 'toilet' breaks, during which she seems to acquire an even stronger Lambert & Butler stench).

Gary usually works on the till to the left of me. He is at college doing a course in I'm not sure what, because he mumbles and I can never understand a word he is saying. He has mousy coloured, bouffy hair and although he has tried to go for the Harry Styles 2012 look, it is more Ronald Macdonald. His eyes are too close together and he has a mole, rather like a Coco Pop, on the end of his chin. He never speaks to the customers, just grunts and keeps his head down. He shoves their items into the Wilko carrier bag (which will inevitably split as soon as they leave the store) then pushes it towards them whilst making strange guttural noises. Our manager is called Robin, he is a beer bellied jobs worth who seems to think he is running the world rather than a substandard version of Woolworths.

I'm not on the tills today, I am on the shop floor watching old ladies look for Rich Tea biscuits and bunion plasters, fat balding men in the DIY section (it is so obvious they'll fuck up whatever is they're building or mending and their wives will shout at them) and little kids putting their dirty fingers in the Pick n Mix (little bastards and their germs have prevented me helping myself to the Strawberry Bon Bons and Fizzy Jelly Bears!) I'm in aisle number seven watching a teenage boy in a hoodie shove rolls of Pritt Stick into his pocket when I hear a voice behind me. Before I turn, I think that it would be far more interesting if Pritt Stick boy was wearing a tweed blazer and named Tarquin.

"Miss Stevens, what a nice surprise."

I turn around and Christopher Green is standing there wearing a cream chunky knit jumper, jeans and walking boots. This bloke has really lost his swagger today, laughs my subconscious. Doesn't he realise that this is Penge High Street, not the Peak District- he looks a right wally in those walking boots, and don't get me started on the jumper, he looks like an extra from Emmerdale.

"I was in the area and there are a few things I need," he continues. He purchases some masking tape, rope, overalls, and cable ties. I can't work out whether he is going to be doing some home improvements or acting out a scene from American Psycho- all he needs is the nail gun. While I am fetching the items for him, we discuss the article and I mention that we could do with some original photos of him, unbelievably he agrees to do a photo shoot. He seems to have far too much spare time on his hands. My friend Juan is a photographer, so I take Christopher's business card and agree to call him to arrange the shoot.

What happens next is all as far-fetched as what has happened so far, so I will give you the condensed version. Kayleigh, Juan and I all go to Christopher's hotel the next day to do the photo shoot. After the shoot, Christopher asks me to go for a coffee with him, which I accept (I'm a student, I've gottta make the most of a free breakfast when I can). After coffee we walk down the road together and I nearly get run over by some nutter on a motorbike who is speeding, luckily Christopher is there to save me and I find myself in his arms. He gazes into my eyes and it is all very perfume advert sexual tension, but he doesn't kiss me and I'm worried whether I have nostril hairs sticking out, bad breath or crud in the corner of my mouth. Either way, I am convinced he doesn't fancy me.

The next day he sends me some books. They're a bit shit (I would have preferred chocolates) and I'm tempted to sell them on eBay. Instead Kayleigh, Juan and I go to the student union bar and get shit-faced. Whilst at the bar I phone Christopher to ask him why he sent me the books, he asks me if I'm drunk and he says he's coming to the bar to get me. I wonder how the hell he is going to do that, I haven't even told him where I am. Perhaps he has a James Bond style gadget, which can find my exact location at the touch of a button. Oooh perhaps he is James Bond! I ponder over which one I'd prefer... Sean Connery- too hairy, Roger Moore- only one facial expression, Timothy Dalton- receding hairline, Daniel Craig- too short, Pierce Brosnan- too orange, George Lazenby- who? Maybe he's some type of super hero and he'll turn up in the Batmobile (I do hope he comes circa Christian Bale or Val Kilmer, not Adam West- all fat belly and grey tights. And I do hope he doesn't bring Robin with him, two's company and all that). Or maybe he's Superman, although I'm not really keen on the whole pants over tights look- must get really sweaty balls too in all that Lycra.

Anyway, somehow Christopher does turn up, right at the point where a drunken Juan is trying to shove his tongue down my throat outside the bar. Oh and did I mention that I throw up? Yep, right in front of this gorgeous man, I re-enact the pea soup scene from the Exorcist (except I've been drinking cider and Sambuca shots so it's not quite so green). You would think that this would send him running for the hills, but no far from it; the next morning I wake up in Christopher Green's hotel bed (we didn't shag thank God; I haven't shaved my legs in over a week, and I have a layer of stubble worse than a tranny).

We have breakfast, he tells me about his helicopter, I meet some weird bloke called Tyler who always seems to be lurking in or around Christopher's suite, then it is time for me to leave and here we are.

Chapter 3- The First Kiss

The lift arrives and we step inside. Thankfully it is a far cry from the usual lifts I travel in, for starters it doesn't stink of piss and it is free from the standard graffiti of random pictures of penises, 'Tony 4 Claire' and 'your mum sucks dicks' scrawled across the walls. Instead it is pretty much as one would expect from a posh hotel; clean and working. We're alone and suddenly there is this inexplicable electricity between us. My heart thumps and my breathing quickens. Christopher turns his head towards me and his eyes darken and smoulder, gazing at me with fierce intensity. I bite my bottom lip (which I really must stop doing as I've pierced the skin and a little scab is beginning to form) as my heart feels as though it will burst through my chest.

"Oh, fuck the paperwork," he breathes. He suddenly dives towards me, pushing me up against the elevator wall (had he done this in the type of lifts I frequent, there would be chewing gum or some other suspect looking gunge sticking to my hair). Before I can even comprehend what is happening, he's holding both of my hands above my head and his hips are pushing against me. Blood is pumping through my body and the anticipation is just too much. But then, I am suddenly aware that my armpits are right in his face. Oh Bollocks! I begin to panic; did I use my anti-white mark deodorant, or is he getting a rancid view of a yellowish white crust along the underarm of my vest top? I remember shaving my armpits in a hurry this morning and I'm praying that I haven't got five o'clock shadow under my arms.

His free hand grabs at my face and quickly his lips are on mine and as I moan into his mouth, his tongue slips in. My inner goddess has a look on her face as though she is about to heave and as her nose wrinkles in disgust I remember; I haven't brushed my teeth. Flashbacks of vomiting into the azaleas outside the club make an unwanted appearance into my head.

You bloody idiot! shrieks my subconscious, sneering at me. *You stay the night at Mr Drop-Dead Gorgeous' house, he leans in for a snog (and let's face it Luv, you don't get many of those) and you have to go and spoil it all with your sicky morning breath!* I really don't need any of her shit right now, what did she expect me to do? I had no idea I wouldn't be returning home when I left the house, and as I'm still a twenty-one-year-old-virgin, it's not like I carry a spare toothbrush in my handbag in case I get lucky on random nights out. What is her problem, surely she didn't expect me to use his toothbrush- not only would that be taking liberties, considering I hardly know him, but it is also rather gross. His teeth may look nice but who knows whether he has Gingivitis, Periodontitis or nasty mouth ulcers.

Chapter 4 – The Build Up

So it turns out that my flatmate Kayleigh, is now seeing Christopher's brother Ellis; they met at the student union on the night of vomitgate and ended up snogging on the dance floor. Ellis is fit, but not as fit as his brother. His most unattractive feature is his catch-phrase of 'laters baby'. The first time I heard him say it, my subconscious was not happy, she tut-tutted and wagged her finger. Laters baby, laters baby- who says that? Oh no, I bet he high fives, air quotes, gives people the thumbs up and does the 'peace sign' in photos too. When I arrive back at the flat, Ellis is there practically eating Kayleigh's face off. It is clear from her bird's nest hair and red face that he stayed over and they've been up all night shagging. She is such a dirty slut. Hmm, now now Annabella, just cos you're not getting any and you're starting to get cobwebs between your legs, there's really no need to be bitter.

That night Christopher takes me for a ride in his helicopter. Yes you heard correctly, his helicopter. Most girls have to make do with a quick fumble in the back of a Fiat, after they've been treated to a slap up meal at Wetherspoons (a Harvester complete with all you can eat salad bar if he's really trying to impress).

Fifty Hues of Hairy Legs and Morning Breath

Afterwards we go back to his apartment, for he has something he wants to show me which will apparently make me want to run for the hills. On our way to the apartment I think of all the things it could possibly be. The state of his bedroom perhaps-empty takeaway boxes with mould growing in them left by the bed, underpants with wank stains strewn on the floor, copies of Playboy with various pages stuck together shoved down the back of his chest of drawers. Maybe he's a real nerd and wants to show me his stamp or badge collection. What if he has Spiderman bed covers and matching curtains? Supposing, Annabella don't even think it, it would be too horrific. Supposing he is a... a... Scientologist?!

When I eventually find out what it is, I am hugely relieved to discover that it is not his badge collection, and that his biggest idol is not Tom Cruise. He leads me into a room with dark burgundy walls and ceiling. I wonder whether I should tell him that magnolia or apple white would have really helped to open up the room and create the illusion of space. Then I notice a large wooden cross shaped like an X fastened to a wall and I am perplexed; he's a Bible Basher? On the other side of the room I spot paddles, whips and riding crops, how can he possibly have time for horse riding what with all the helicopter flying? In the middle of the room is a huge bed, I guess all the horse riding and preaching must be pretty exhausting. Other items in the room include ropes, chains, shackles and some weird looking thing with tiny plastic beads on the end; hmmm it seems odd that he keeps a toilet brush when there isn't a toilet in here.

"Are you going to say anything?" Christopher asks.

I'm not really sure what to say. Perhaps I should tell him that I'm an Atheist, don't really like burgundy and I'm not a fan of jodhpurs. Oh for Christ's sake Annabella, get with the programme, this is a sex room. He's into S&M, he wants to bring you in here and slap your sorry arse with what you mistook for a toilet brush.

So just to reiterate, Christopher Green wants me to be his submissive. He wants to use his riding crop to hit me and get this, he not only wants me to sign a non-disclosure agreement, but he also wants me to sign a contract to say that I agree to the terms and conditions of being his submissive! Suddenly the Scientology doesn't seem so bad after all. The cheeky, presumptuous fucker has even brought the contract with him. I take a very brief glance over it.

"So, are there any sexual acts you feel uncomfortable doing?" Christopher asks.

"Well, I've never actually done any of them, I've never had sex."

"Um, what, are you telling me that you are a virgin?"

Fifty Hues of Hairy Legs and Morning Breath

Silence.

"You're a virgin?" he asks again, open mouthed and eyes wide. He rubs his brow in exasperation, then shakes his head frantically.

"Why the fuck didn't you say anything?!" he bellows.

I open my mouth to speak, then quickly shut it again. I have no idea what to say to him. How do I tell this hunk that I've never played Spin the Bottle, never had a drunken fumble on holiday with a Spanish Waiter called Miguel, never given my boyfriend a quick wank whilst babysitting the neighbour's kids, never had a friend with (albeit rather mediocre) benefits and never let Jason from down the road, finger me at the party Mandy had when her parents were away. How on earth am I supposed to explain to this gorgeous man, that my knowledge of all things sexual is pretty much on a par with a Tibetan Monk's?

He turns his head towards me, his eyes narrowing. "Please don't tell me that I'm the first man who has kissed you?"

I splutter, "God no, don't be silly. I've kissed loads of guys." My subconscious snorts, guffaws of laughter of erupting from her. Pah, you wish! Pizza-faced Gary who kissed like a Gecko, and weasely Ian who left half a ton of slobber over your face and that piece of chicken in your mouth you horrifyingly dislodged from his teeth- you're hardly Samantha Jones are you?! Although she is highly irritating, she does have a point. I glance at Christopher sheepishly. "Shall I leave?"

"What? No, I don't want you to leave."

"But you seem really mad with me," I mumble shyly.

"I'm not mad, I'm just very surprised Annabella."

I look down at the floor, embarrassed.

"Please stop biting your lip," he says, his voice a low throaty whisper. Sounds a bit like one of those phone perverts who asks what colour knickers you're wearing, remarks my subconscious.

I quickly glance up- I wasn't even aware I was biting my lip. What's his problem, it's not as if it's one of my worst habits. It's a good job he didn't catch me picking my nose (I'm a flicker, not a roller) or using a hairclip to clean under my toenails then placing the said hairclip back in my hair, or picking my split ends, or squeezing the puss out of ingrown hairs and getting really quite excited when the curly, wiggly hair eventually pokes through... I am interrupted from my train of thought by my subconscious who clears her throat loudly. God Annabella you really are rank, what on earth does he see in you? My inner goddess is equally unimpressed and is dry retching with a Kleenex over her mouth and nose.

"Sorry, I wasn't aware I was biting my lip, and I didn't realised it irritated you quite so much," I mutter apologetically.

"It doesn't irritate me," Christopher replies. "Quite the opposite in fact. I want to bite it too." He looks at me sensually, his grey eyes boring deep into me. Suddenly my inner goddess has perked up; gone are the Kleenex and dry retching; she's got her batty riders on and is doing the Dutty Wine, bumping and grinding on the dance floor in a highly provocative way.

"Come Annabella," murmurs Christopher, holding out his hand to me.

"Huh?"

"We're going to rectify this problem right now."

"Problem, what problem?"

"Your problem Annabella. I'm going to make love to you, now."

My inner goddess suddenly grinds to a halt mid Boogie. The sexy, rhythmic dancehall music is replaced with Cliff Richard's greatest hits and she has on a pair of beige, elasticated-around-the-waist slacks, Scholl sandals and a brown anorak. I am highly disappointed, I didn't expect Mr 'I'm so sexually experienced and erotic' Green to completely ruin the moment by telling me he was going to 'make love to me'. I may not know a great deal about sex, but I was rather hoping it would be more of a passionate, throw-everything-off-of-the-table-in-one-swift-motion and take me there and then kind of affair.

His huge bedroom has ceiling-height windows which look out over the twinkling lights of Chelsea Harbour. I take a deep breath, trying to control my breathing and attempt to stop my body from shaking. This is it; I am finally going to lose my virginity. I am going to lose my virginity to a stunning millionaire! Unbelievable eh?

I watch him as he removes his watch and places it on top of a chest of drawers that matches the bed, then removes his jacket and places it on a chair. My subconscious nudges me, you've got to be kidding me, she says disparagingly. What's wrong with this dude, OCD or what? I mean c'mon, millionaire or no millionaire he's still a bloke. Surely that watch should be thrown at the chest of drawers a little too forcefully, so that it either falls down the back of it joining his porn collection, bits of fluff, an apple core and odd socks, or so that it hits the surface resulting in it breaking- the watch that is, not the chest of drawers- he's a millionaire after all, so I'll bet he didn't get it from Ikea and take three hours to put it up whilst swearing and accidently hammering his fingers. And don't get me started on the jacket- placing it on a chair, as opposed to just tossing it on the floor next to a pair of crusty underpants and damp, slightly musty towel. Seriously this guy is a freak- I'll bet he even puts the toilet seat down! Trying my best to ignore her, I gaze at Christopher- he really is breathtakingly beautiful. His unruly dark copper hair is mussed and his eyes sparkle intensely. Dark Copper, laughs my subconscious cruelly, oh come on pull the other one, he's ginger and you know it!

He steps out of his Converse shoes and reaches down to take his socks off individually. Christopher Green's feet... Eurgh, what is it about naked feet? My inner goddess is trying not to look, she is repulsed by the alien-like, long hairy toes and the thick, ridged toenails that look like they haven't seen nail clippers in weeks.

Chapter 5 - The Sex

Christopher slowly glides towards me and begins to unbutton my shirt. Gradually he peels it off me and lets it fall to the floor. He stands back and gazes appreciatively at me. Well this is all very well, interrupts my subconscious, but what happens when he takes that gel-filled bra that weighs about twenty kilos off and realises that your tits resemble two fried eggs? Oh well, no turning back now.

"Oh Annabella", he breathes. "You have the most beautiful skin, pale and flawless. I want to..." You wait until you see the large red zit on her back, my subconscious giggles maliciously, it is minging! It's in one of those awkward places where you can't squeeze it and it's filled with yellow pus. I ignore the bitch and just hope that his hands don't stray to my back; she's right, it is gross. Christopher grasps my hair tie, pulls it free and gasps as my hair cascades around my shoulders. Oh no, why's he gasping, have I got that funny mushroom shape that you get when you've had your hair tied up all day? Can he spy dandruff?

"I like Brunettes," he murmurs and both of his hands are in my hair grasping each side of my head. He kisses me fervently, his tongue exploring my mouth. His hands slowly glide down my lower back along to my bum, and I automatically tense my body; shit, he's going to be able to feel my cellulite through my jeans. Luckily my cratered bum hasn't put him off and he pulls me even closer to him so that I can feel his erection pushing against me. My inner goddess has her batty riders back on and she's shaking her arse and hips like someone from a 50 Cent video. Gripping his upper arms, I feel his biceps, which he obviously flexes as soon as I touch them.

Suddenly he drops to his knees and gazes up at me through his impossibly long lashes. Hmm I wonder if he dyes them, my subconscious ponders. Well come on Annabella, he is very metrosexual. Ooh, maybe he's wearing manscara! I almost tell her to piss off out loud, but I'm distracted by Christopher's hands reaching up to undo the zip on my jeans. Uh oh, sniggers my subconscious, looks like the scaffolding is about to come off; your arse is going to wobble all over the place like a sallow Panna Cotta. He leans forward and runs his nose up the apex between my thighs. I feel him. There. Oh for God's sake Annabella! My subconscious' tone is scolding. You can say it y'know, it's called a Fanny, you don't need to be so bashful about it.

"You smell so good." He murmurs and closes his eyes. I am relieved that I used my Body Shop shower gel down there and squeezed in an extra bit of Summer Breeze Lenor when I washed my underwear. He pushes me gently so that I fall onto the bed. He pulls off my shoes, followed by my socks and runs his thumbnail up my instep. It is extremely ticklish and I have to try really hard to suppress my giggles, as I don't want to ruin the moment. My inner goddess is clearly not impressed with the foot caressing and has slowed down her bumping and grinding. He runs his tongue along my instep and my inner goddess gags. God he's brave, he obviously hasn't spotted that crusty patch of skin on your heel. I told you that JML Ped Egg was a waste of money, nothing is going to make those bad boys baby smooth, sneers my subconscious.

"You're very beautiful, Annabella Stevens. I can't wait to be inside you."

For the first time, I am beginning to panic. He's going to be inside me. The only things that have been inside me are a tampon and a bit of Germolene that accidentally found its way there- don't ask, I got my pubes caught in the zip of my jeans once, drew blood and everything, bloody agony it was.

"Show me how you pleasure yourself."

I frown and in my head begin to list all my pleasurable past-times; eating a whole tub of Ben & Jerry's whilst watching Vampire Diaries, getting completely shit-faced with my best friend and singing 'Achy Breaky Heart' at Karaoke, picking out all the bobbly ones from a packet of Liquorice Allsorts, then squishing them together and cramming them all into my mouth at once whilst attempting to burp the entire alphabet.

No you idiot, interrupts my subconscious, not those kind of pleasures- sexual pleasures.

"Don't be coy Annabella, show me," he whispers.

I shake my head at him.

"How do you make yourself come? I want to see." Before I even have time to think, my subconscious is lecturing me. Before you say 'come where' like a bloody fool, he means sex Annabella- he's talking about an orgasm.

"I don't," I mumble sheepishly and I feel my cheeks burning with embarrassment.

"Well we'll have to see what we can do about that," he replies and without taking his eyes off mine he undoes the buttons of his jeans and slowly pulls them down. He leans over me and grasping each of my ankles jerks my legs apart and climbs onto the bed between my legs. I am absolutely, bloody terrified. Suppose it hurts? What if I bleed all over his sheets, or even to death! What am I supposed to do, do I just lie still or should I wriggle about a bit? Am I supposed to make those 'Oooh, aaah' noises and heavy breathing sounds that I've seen on T.V?

He trails a line of kisses from my belly and his tongue dips into my navel (thankfully, although I have an innie as opposed to an outie, it's not too innie so as to gather belly button fluff). Christopher lies down beside me and his hand moves up towards my breasts. Panic erupts inside me as his hand curls round to cup my left tit.

"You fit my hand perfectly Annabella," he murmurs. Yeah well wait till that bra comes off, laughs my subconscious, you'll be well disappointed, there's not enough boob there to fill a squirrel monkey's hand. I do my best to ignore her, but I am still petrified as his index finger slips into the cup of my bra and pulls it down to reveal my breast. My breasts swell and my nipples harden, I have no idea what the hell is going on- my nipples only do this when I'm cold and I'm certainly not cold right now. He pulls down the other bra cup and I'm trussed up by my own bra. I feel ridiculous; rather like a turkey with the string tied round it.

"Very nice." he whispers appreciatively, clearly he is not put off by tits that resemble two bee stings.

He blows very gently on one and although I am wondering why he feels the need to cool my nipple down, I have to say it does feel rather nice. His hand moves to my other breast and his fingers knead the nipple gently. It's a nice sensation; one which I can feel all the way down to my groin and I realise there is a wetness in between my legs. For a split second alarm kicks in as I think I have peed myself, but I realise that the feeling is different and there isn't that emptiness you get in your bladder after doing a wee; in fact, this feeling doesn't seem to be connected to my bladder.

Suddenly his mouth is around one of my nipples and he is licking and sucking as though it is a lollipop.

"Let's see if we can make you come like this." he says. I don't understand; he wants me to have an orgasm, I thought you had an orgasm during sex, are we having sex? Is all this nipple sucking and blowing malarkey sex? Is this it?! Surely this can't be what all the fuss is about, I mean it's nice and all, but is this what I've waited twenty one years for?

Just as I start to think that this is it, that I've lost my virginity, his hand moves down to my waist, to my hips and then it is between my legs. His fingers move towards my knickers and I am glad I ditched my comfy flesh coloured ones in favour of white lace. His fingers slip under the lace and before I know it he has put one inside me. Whilst my inner goddess is opening and closing her legs, flashing her minge at everyone a la Sharon Stone, I am wondering what I must feel like to him; does it feel gross, all wet and slimy like sticking your hand up a chicken?

My thoughts are interrupted as Christopher sits up and tugs my knickers off. Oh no, he's going to see it. I hope he doesn't look at it too closely, I really won't feel comfortable having someone peering at it. I trimmed my pubic hair this morning but I have no idea if I've done it right; my flatmate Kayleigh said I should go for something called a Hollywood wax, which apparently removes all of the hair down there- is she fucking crazy!! I once had my legs waxed and the pain was so bad I thought I was going to die. So I'm afraid Christopher will have to do with a trim; it doesn't look too bad, but I really don't understand why when my head hair is straight, my pubic hair is so curly.

Christopher pulls off his boxer briefs and there it is... his penis. Jesus Christ, it's huge! How the hell is that going to fit inside my little hole? I am really starting to panic as I remember how painful it was the first time I inserted a tampon, this thing in front of me is at least twice as big. My inner goddess is cowering behind the sofa with her hands over her eyes, she peeks between a gap in her fingers at the long veiny monster and gasps in horror, covering her eyes again. I look at his penis once more and I am surprised by how ugly it is- Kayleigh did not prepare me for this. The tip is an angry looking reddish purple and the shaft resembles a piece of raw meat. Although I've heard that willies aren't particularly attractive, I'm still surprised, especially when I look at the wrinkly skin around the testicles. Oh get over yourself scolds my subconscious, your fanny hardly resembles Aphrodite does it? Point well made.

Christopher has reached over to the bedside table and is now taking a condom out of its packet. I pray that he doesn't ask me to put it on him; the last time I touched a condom was in Miss McKenzie's PSHE class in Year 10. We were supposed to practise putting them on a banana (I remember that even though I was the least sexually aware in the class, even I knew that if your penis resembled a banana then either you've got a severe case of jaundice or it is time for a trip to the GUM clinic) but we spent most of our time blowing them up, or trying to stretch them over our heads, much to Miss McKenzie's frustration. Thankfully I needn't have worried and Christopher has rolled the condom over his penis.

"Don't worry," he says, obviously sensing my anxiety. "You expand too." He makes my fanny sound like a marshmallow in the microwave.

He leans down with his hands either side of my head and it's only now that I register that he's still wearing his shirt. Thank heavens it's not his socks; Kayleigh advised me about that. "If you look down and he's still got his socks on, make your excuses, get your clothes on and get out of there quick!" She'd warned. "If he keeps his socks on during sex, there's no end to what he'll do; wear a fleece, own a bum bag, wear novelty ties, have a secret stash of Christmas jumpers, Hawaiian shirts, thermal vests and he'll probably come in about five seconds."

"Pull your knees up." Christopher orders softly. "I'm going to fuck you now Miss Stevens." He positions the head of his erection at the entrance of my sex. NO, NO, NO! shrieks my subconscious. If you keep calling it that you'll never get any! Fanny, Muff, Pussy, Minge, Vajayjay, Poonani, you can even use the C word if you like, but please for God's sake you will promise never to call it your Sex again- you are not living in the 18th Century.

His penis has slammed into me and I cry out loud as I feel a weird pinching sensation deep inside me.

"You're so tight. You okay?"

Tight, I am not tight. I got a round of drinks at the student union bar last week. I gave the waitress in Nando's a two quid tip yesterday! I'll give him tight, bloody cheek! My subconscious gives me a loud exaggerated sigh. He means your fanny Annabella, your fanny is tight.

"I'm going to move baby." he whispers.

"Ok," I reply and he thrusts into me again.

"More?"

"Yes." I breathe and he thrusts again and again and again. As I grow accustomed to the feeling, I begin to move my hips up to meet his. His breathing is loud and quick and as he comes he calls out my name. He slowly pulls out of me then leans down to kiss my forehead.

"How was it?" he asks, gazing at me with his beautiful eyes.

I smile at him and as I start to roll over so that I can place my arm around him, it happens. A long, loud eruption, like a Whoopee Cushion has gone off in between my legs. The thing that Kayleigh warned me could happen but assured me it would be most unlikely. The Fanny Fart.

My inner goddess is the colour of a beef tomato, her eyes are open wide in horror as she takes a step backward and very slowly, the ground opens up and swallows her.

Chapter 6 - The Piano

When I wake up it is dark and I have no idea how long I've been asleep for; long enough for morning breath, bed hair and panda eyes? Luckily Christopher is nowhere to be seen, so I throw the covers off, leap out of bed and dash over to the mirror. Hmmm, my hair is scraggly and matted like a bird's nest, the mascara is smudged and amongst the clumped lashes is yellow eye bogey. Now time for the breath test; Jesus Christ! My mouth smells like I have been licking a tramp's bum crack. I lean over to the bedside table and grab my handbag, reaching around inside I find some loose change, a chewed pen lid, lip balm, deodorant and a bit of fluff but no chewing gum. Shit.

I run into the bathroom and lock the door behind me so that should Christopher make a re-appearance, he won't be able to come in and find me looking and smelling like shit. I rummage around in his bathroom cabinet and find mouthwash and dental floss. Once the breath is sorted, I run my fingers through my hair in an attempt to smooth out the pillow frizz. A bit of damp loo roll sorts out the eye bogey and most of the mascara.

By the time I have finished in the bathroom there is still no sign of Christopher, I walk towards the bedroom door and as I do so, I hear the faint sound of music. With the duvet wrapped around me, I walk down the corridor towards the big room.

Christopher is at the piano playing a beautiful melody, he sits naked. Whoa there, shrieks my subconscious, naked piano playing in the middle of the night, seriously?! What is wrong with this guy?

I watch his long skilled fingers gently tap the keys and as I do so, I can't help but wonder whether he has washed his hands; after all, I know where those fingers have been. He glances up.

"Sorry," I whisper. "I didn't mean to disturb you."

"Surely I should be saying that to you," he replies.

He's got a point actually, he's the one making all the noise with his random naked piano playing.

He finishes playing and puts his hand on his legs and that's when I notice that in actual fact he is not naked. Just as I'm about to take a deep breath of relief that the man I have just had sex with is not a freaky naked piano player, I realise that in fact something far, far worse is happening. He is wearing pyjama bottoms. Whaaaaaaaat, yells my subconscious, fear and panic evident in her voice, Pyjama bottoms?! Oh. My. God. And they're striped, is this guy seventy five? My inner goddess is equally unhappy; she has taken off her crotch-less panties and satin corset and is wearing a grubby towelling dressing gown and matching slippers. I try to distract myself from the pyjama bottoms (oh please God don't let them be from Marks & Spencer).

"You play the piano beautifully, how long have you been playing?"

"Since I was six."

My subconscious suppresses a cough. Jeez, what a geek, she says rudely and a small part of me can't help but agree. I go back to bed and quickly fall asleep. My sleep is filled with nightmares of a ginger bloke playing Bach in the buff.

Chapter 7 - The Toilet

As light begins to fill the room, I wake from a deep sleep. I roll over to face Christopher Green who is still asleep; his full, pouty lips are slightly parted and as I lean in closer to him I get a waft of morning breath- not full on dragon breath but slightly dog-like. My inner goddess wrinkles her nose and waves her little hand in front of her face to show her disgust at the lack of minty-freshness. I decide against planting a kiss on his lips. Instead I gaze at him, his hair is an absolute mess and Worzel Gummidge without his Handsome Head springs to mind. (Yes, yes I know I am only twenty one and therefore shouldn't have a clue who Worzel Gummidge is, but if people will believe the line 'he pours himself into me as he finds his release' despite the fact that 'he' is wearing a condom, then I think I'm entitled to at least one unrealistic line!)

Despite the breath and Fraggle Rock hair, he is still gorgeous and I could stare at him forever, but nature calls and I'm desperate for a pee. I peel the covers off slowly so that I don't wake him and gently slip out of the bed. I spy his shirt on the floor and put it on to cover my naked body. I enter his huge bathroom and sit on the toilet smiling in relief as I empty my bladder. But my smile is short lived, deep in my belly I can feel gurgling and that heavy sensation in my bowels which can only mean one thing... I'm going to have to shit in his house!

Beads of sweat begin to prick on my forehead as panic sets in. I can't believe my body is doing this to me, I don't even poo in the university loos, let alone in the house of the fittest man I have ever met. Just as I wonder whether I can hold it until I get home, my stomach makes a groaning sound and I can feel the pressure building up inside- not only do I need to shit but it's going to be a loud and knowing my luck, smelly one. I don't have much time to act; I leap off the toilet and begin searching through his bathroom cabinet in search of something which will mask the inevitable eggy stench, I find a can of some expensive looking deodorant which will have to do.

Now to try and reduce the noise; I lean over to the sink and turn on one of the taps, then I begin to unravel the toilet roll. I stop at eight sheets, I need enough to line the bottom of the toilet to prevent the plopping noise, but not so much that I end up blocking it. Taking my wad of toilet roll I reach down into the toilet bowl, I assess the situation and reach for five more sheets of paper. Oh come on Annabella interrupts my subconscious every bloke knows the toilet-roll-stuffed-down-the-bottom-of-the-loo-to-try-and-disguise-the-sound-of-you-taking-a-dump trick; the decreased size of the roll of loo paper and having to flush the toilet twice are a dead giveaway. Although I know she is right, I still add the extra five sheets to my wad and lay it at the bottom of the toilet.

Fifty Hues of Hairy Legs and Morning Breath

I sit down on the toilet, and a huge fart, followed by what feels like an elephant poo, make their exits. The smell, whilst a little whiffy, is not too bad, so I only need a quick spray of the deodorant. I stand up to wipe myself and am horrified to discover that it is one of those poos where one or two wipes is just not enough- fuck it, this means more toilet roll thus more potential for toilet blockage. As I pull the handle down to flush the toilet, I take a deep breath... I am relieved to find that the toilet flushes normally and there is no trace of my ever having done a poo. Christopher Green can continue to think that I am a sexy woman who doesn't burp, pick my nose or shit. Hurrah!

Chapter 8 - Oral

The bath tub is huge and luxurious. Flash git, sneers my subconscious. I watch Christopher pour expensive looking bath oil into the water. Oh great, I'll be slipping and sliding all over the bloody place, supposing I fall arse over tit as I climb in, he's already seen me puke my guts up- I really don't think I can handle any more embarrassment. Christopher pulls his T-shirt over his head and throws it onto the floor. Typical, him trying to impress me with his tidiness and cleanliness didn't last long. I guess it'll only be a matter of time before he's farting in bed, taking a dump while I'm brushing my teeth and eating Pot Noodle in his underpants (that he's worn for three days in a row). My inner goddess is scowling at the crumpled T-shirt and tutting at his act of untidiness. I have to resist the urge to pick up the garment and fold it neatly over the towel rail.

"Miss Stevens." He holds his hand out to me. Why must he insist on calling me by my last name? It makes me sound like a school teacher, which is just wrong on so many levels. It conjures up an image of my science teacher; she had coffee breath, a hairy chin and was slightly cross-eyed. Not sexy.

I dip my toe into the water, it is too damn hot and I know that in about five minutes I am going to have prune skin, frizzy hair and a bright red face. I smile sweetly at him, while effing and blinding inwards. As I sink into the water, gritting my teeth as the hot water hits my fanny, Christopher reaches for a bottle of body wash. I eye it with suspicion; this is not my usual bath routine. I am used to having my shower radio in the room with me so that I can sing along, loudly and tunelessly, to whatever cheesy songs may be playing on the radio. I have also failed to body brush before entering the water, something I do religiously, as I read in a magazine once that it improves circulation and cellulite. Ha! Give me a break, screams my subconscious, you'll believe any old shit you read in those crappy magazines of yours. Want to lose the orange peel thighs- try cutting down on the chocolate Luv; you might have a high metabolism now, but by the time you're thirty-five you'll have a backside like a Walrus.

Christopher has begun to lather up the body wash and he is now sitting behind me with his legs stretched out next to mine. He begins to rub my neck, my back then along my sides up to my underarms. My inner goddess recoils in horror- it has been more than twenty four hours since I shaved my armpits, which can only mean one thing… stubble! I instinctively press my arms tightly to my sides in order to prevent him for getting to my arm pits, but it is futile and I feel his fingers trying to prise my arms away from my body.

"Lift your arms up for me baby," he whispers into my ear. "I want to wash you."

Nobody has washed me since I was about five, back in the days when I had bubble bath that turned the water pink and a fairy princess flannel- and I'm a little worried about where this could be heading. I shudder and reluctantly lift my arms. He won't want to touch me with a barge pole after he's discovered that my armpits resemble the bristles of a six foot builder called Pete. Yet I couldn't be more wrong; he clearly has a penchant for rubbing cacti-like skin and I can feel his growing erection against my back.

"Turn around. I need washing too." he murmurs into my ear. What is it with him and washing? The last person I washed was my cousin Frankie who is three; I had to clean the dried bogey from around his nostrils, rid his ears of what looked like a mixture of Marmite and peanut butter and it took me a good few scrubs with the sponge to get the rather suspect looking gunge out from in between his toes. I am therefore hoping that washing Christopher will be a far more pleasant experience. I pause for a second to think about how I can turn to face him in the most ladylike fashion, without slipping and sloshing water everywhere. When I turn to face him, I discover that he is holding his penis firmly in his hands. The top of it is above the water line and I have to stifle a giggle; it really does look quite ridiculous, bobbing about in the water like a misshapen Frankfurter.

Christopher is staring deep into my eyes and I can tell he wants me to touch it. I guess I'd better get on with it before the water makes my fingers all wrinkly. He closes his eyes as I move my hand up and down the shaft. He moans in pleasure and it suddenly dawns on me that he is going to expect me to do it; to perform oral sex on him, to give him a blow job. I've always mused over why they say 'perform' oral sex- why is it a performance? Should I dress up in a costume and stage makeup? Will he applaud at the end? Will I get a standing ovation? Are people going to buy tickets to come and watch? Should I do 'Jazz Hands'? Hmmm, maybe not. For once my subconscious doesn't stick her oar in, for she knows that I am only joking; I may be naive when it comes to sex but I'm not completely stupid. The term 'blow job', on the other hand, is another matter and I have to admit I had to get some clarification from Kayleigh.

"So remember," she had said to me as we sat in our PJs eating ice cream. "You don't actually blow on it, or up it, you put it in your mouth and suck it," she had explained.

Despite Kayleigh's words of wisdom I am still terrified. Am I going to get his pubic hairs stuck in between my teeth, or even down my throat? How hard should I suck- should I imagine it's a strawberry Calypso and give it a firm suck, or a Mint Magnum and just lick round the edges? And what do I do with my teeth; what happens if I accidentally nip it, or even bite it off! What do I do if it tastes gross, will I end up retching?

I look at Christopher, who still has his eyes closed. Right, I'm just going to go for it. If I completely bugger it up, I'll just have to run out of this apartment and hope I never see him again. I can leave town, or even the country, to avoid bumping into him. If I do happen to accidentally bite it, I'll just have to hope he doesn't bleed to death. How will I explain that to the authorities? I could always say he got it stuck in his zip, or he was cooking naked and caught it on the tin opener.

While he still has his eyes closed, I lean forward and put my lips over his penis and suck cautiously; it is certainly no Mint Magnum, but neither is it as gross as I imagined it to be. Christopher gasps in surprise as I move up and down with my lips tightly pursed around his erection. I continue the movement, and when I look up to take another sneaky peek at him I see it… His sex face. Jesus Christ, what a troll! My inner goddess has regurgitated last night's meatballs as she stares in horror at the face that has taken on the expression of someone either trying to win the gurning championships or squeeze out an almighty shit.

Just as I feel as though I am going to lose my rhythm, I feel Christopher reach up to my hair and pull my head forward so that he is deeper in my mouth. I can feel him right at the back of my throat and it is a most unpleasant sensation, almost like when you are scraping your tongue and go a little too far back. I try and pull away a bit, but his grip tightens and he is deep at the back of my throat again; what the hell is he doing? Is he trying to find out whether I've had my tonsils removed? Jeez, he could just ask. Is he trying to kill me; death by dick? Once more I try and pull away so that I can actually breathe, but once again he pushes himself deeper into me. If he does not stop I am going to fucking bite it on purpose, either that or I will throw up all over it. I wonder how he would like it if I took a Walls sausage and shoved it whole down his oesophagus.

Suddenly his face contorts even more (that is **so not a good look**, remarks my subconscious in Gok Wan mode) and the next thing I know, my mouth is full of something warm and salty tasting which has a rather phlegm-like texture. I try not to retch and quickly swallow. He could have bloody warned me-selfish prick. He opens his eyes and gazes at me, a look of contentment on his face.

"Wow, that was amazing."

Camille R. Harding

I can't help but smile, for although up until yesterday I had never even seen a willy, let alone put one in my mouth, I am apparently an expert at blow jobs- unbelievable eh?

I still would have preferred the Mint Magnum though.

Chapter 9 - The Mother

Christopher and I are lying in bed, having just done some very dirty things. My inner goddess is extremely pleased with herself, she is strutting around singing Rod Stewart's 'If You Think I'm Sexy'. My subconscious is kissing her teeth and looking her up and down like she is something on the bottom of her shoe seriously girlfriend, Rod Stewart- not cool. Why couldn't you have chosen 'Sexyback', at least Justin Timberlake is hot and please, if you really must sing learn more than two lines. Personally I think it could be a lot worse; she could be singing Colour Me Badd's 'I Wanna Sex You Up', George Michael's 'I Want Your Sex' or Tom Jones' 'Sex Bomb' complete with bad hair, eighties leather trousers and drunk uncle at a wedding dance moves.

Suddenly my thoughts are interrupted by voices coming from the hallway; it sounds like the creepy guy Tyler and a woman. Christian looks at me in alarm.

"Shit, it's my mother!"

I sit up slowly and rub my eyes, I'm really not a morning person and just want to bury my head under the pillow and go back to sleep.

"Come on Annabella, we need to get dressed- that's if you want to meet my mother."

In actual fact I don't, I have known this guy for all of ten minutes and already he wants me to meet his mother, can't I just hide in here until she's gone? I thought that meeting mothers was something that happened after several months, not days. My mind drifts off and as I picture Christopher and I married, I begin to wonder what type of mother-in-law she might be...

The Clinger:

This is the one that has never really let her baby boy go. She still insists on ruffling his hair and holding his hand at family gatherings. She still calls him revolting pet names like Poppet and Boo Boo, even when he is forty five. She still knits him hideous jumpers for Christmas- and expects him to wear them. Worst of all, she still thinks that it is acceptable for her to spit on a tissue and wipe crumbs away from his mouth.

The Know-it-all:

This is perhaps the worst type, for this one thinks she knows best about everything and anything. This one will interfere in every aspect of your life and will have an opinion on just about every subject, from how to decorate your house, to how to keep your lady garden tidy. She will tell you how to bring up your kids, how to cook, how to clean and how to do your job. This one is so intrusive, that you half expect her head to pop up at the end of the bed during intercourse; "I think it's probably better if you go on top Annabella, that way you can hold on to the head board, really grind your hips down and be sure to get a deeper penetration."

"Oh, no Christopher, I really wouldn't do it like that if I were you; your father and I often find that doggy style is much better on the bed than the floor- I do get terribly sore knees these days and your father's back isn't quite what it used to be."

The Feeder:

The Feeder clearly thinks that you live in Ethiopia and don't have access to supermarkets, restaurants, fridges or freezers. The words 'eat, eat you must eat!' are the ones she is most familiar with. She will bring a casserole with her every time she visits your house (which by the way, is fucking disgusting but you made the silly mistake of telling her ten years ago, out of sheer politeness, that it was delicious and you have had to suffer the consequences of your mistake ever since). If you are feeling poorly she will make a 'nice stew' despite being told five times that you have Gastroenteritis and anything that goes into your stomach will either be projectile vomited out of your mouth, or machine gunned out of your arse.

When you pop round after lunch and therefore remind her that you're not hungry, she replies "Okay then, I'll just make some sandwiches". Her reaction to you telling her that you have been diagnosed with a life threatening illness is to say "Oh you poor love, don't worry I'll go and get some cake from the cupboard". You often wonder whether she is trying to fatten you up so that she can eat you. And woe betide you if you're a Vegetarian; "Don't worry I'll do roast chicken instead of Beef then," a Vegan; "but how do you survive on just nuts," or Lactose intolerant; "Oh don't be silly dear, it's all in the mind."

The Rival:

This one is rather more complex; she wants to be your friend, but at the same time she tries to out-do you on every level. She will try and have lots of things in common with you, even though you are in your twenties and she is in her sixties. She'll want to borrow your clothes even though you're a size eight and she is a size eighteen. She'll be obsessed with your weight because she is jealous; you either need to eat more; "You're looking far too thin, it's not healthy you know", or less; "I see you've got your curves back". She will insist on going shopping with you and you will have to pretend that the floral, pleated, calf-length skirts she picks up in BHS are still in fashion. If you're on a diet, she'll go on one too. If you have a cold, she'll have pneumonia. If you've been diagnosed with heart disease, she'll only have a day to live.

The Critic:

This one is very simple; her attitude is that of 'you're not good enough for my son and you never will be'. She generally thinks that her son is Bollinger and you're Cherry Lambrini.

She'll spend most of the time fawning over her other children's partners whilst making disparaging comments about your hair, clothes, career choice, home keeping skills and cooking. She'll open any gifts you give her with her nose stuck in the air and look at them as though you have handed her a dead rat, then she'll make a remark along the lines of "the quality of the items that you can pick up at these discount stores is very impressive these days".

The Incredibly Dull One:

This one does what it says on the tin; she really is mind-numbingly boring. Her house is full of doilies, Toby Jugs and toilet roll covers. She has tea (or if she's being really wild, sherry) with the vicar. She fills you with useless information along the lines of "I noticed that Jan from number seven has painted her fence", or "did you know that the Co-Op down the road have reduced the price of their Bourbon biscuits?" She makes you want to burst your own ear drums with chop sticks.

The Mutton Dressed As Lamb:

This type, while relatively harmless, is the most embarrassing. She gets absolutely shit-faced at any family event and always tries to kiss your male friends on the mouth. She wears leopard print, low-cut tops which show off her Turkey Neck and crepe cleavage, even though her tits are almost level with her belly button. Her thin, wrinkly old lips will be adorned with bright red or fuchsia lipstick which will usually end up on her teeth. Despite going bald, she dyes her hair jet black or bright orange which only draws even more attention to her ugly, mottled scalp. She wears kitten heeled mules when she should actually be wearing support tights and sensible lace up shoes from Clarks. Even though she has a hacking cough, she still smokes twenty Benson & Hedges a day, which is evident on her nicotine stained fingernails (she has tried to paint them a vamp red, but her cataracts mean she misses most of the time and actually paints her cuticles). She thinks she is young, cool and trendy. You think it was about time she was put in a home…

I am interrupted from my thoughts by voices coming from the living room, one of them female- it's her, the mother.

Christopher leaps off the bed and pulls on his jeans without putting his underwear on. Surely that's got to chafe, scratchy denim rubbing against the skin of the ball bag- I really can't see how that can be comfortable. My inner goddess winces at the thought.

"I have no clean clothes here," I remind him, hoping he'll reconsider the introduction to his mother.

"It's fine," he replies, "you can wear something of mine."

Is he stupid? Wear something of his; does he seriously expect me to meet his mother wearing a bloke's T Shirt and over-sized jeans? I'll look like a right hobo and then she'll definitely be mother-in-law type five.

"Annabella, you'd look beautiful even if you wore a bin liner. I really want you to meet my mother. Get dressed. I'll just go and calm her down." Spooky, it's like he can read my mind, how very Darren Brown.

Calm her down, calm her down, cries my subconscious, well that's hardly reassuring is it?! Why does she need calming down, is she some kind of wild beast? And all this 'mother' business is a bit worrying; why can't he call her mum, mother sounds so old fashioned and stuffy- I bet she's wearing a twin set and pearls. Oh my God, what if she's wearing tweed! She's going to be a right stuck up old bag and she's going to hate you with your man clothes and it's-so-obvious-I've-been-shagging-your-son-hair.

My hands are shaking as I bend down to retrieve my clothes from the floor, thankfully my shirt is relatively crease free and after finding my bra under the bed (where incidentally, there is no porn or empty pizza boxes- this guy must be an alien) I rifle through Christopher's drawers in search of underwear. Please, please don't let me find any Y-Fronts or Long Johns. Luckily his underwear drawer is free from old man Y Fronts, saggy around the bum Long Johns, G strings or novelty boxer shorts and I find a pair of white Calvin Klein's. I pull on my jeans and check that the Calvins haven't given me VPL. There is no obvious VPL, but I look and feel like shit. I'd really like to have a shower, do my hair, put on clean clothes and apply my make up before meeting his or anyone's mother.

I walk into the living room and there she is, standing near the couch. She eyeballs me and I can almost hear her say, "Have you just had sex with my son, you little slut? Don't think you can take him away from me, he'll always love me the most, he'll always be mummy's little boy you know."

I smile sweetly at her but my subconscious is screaming, Ha! Yeah I just screwed your precious little boy and I've seen his sex room- bet you didn't know he was such a dirty perv. And I'm wearing his pants, so there!

"Mother this is Annabella Stevens. Annabella, this is Gretchen Tresilian-Green."

Fifty Hues of Hairy Legs and Morning Breath

Dr Tresilian-Green holds her hand out to me. "It's a pleasure to meet you."

Liar! Shouts my subconscious.

Chapter 10 - The Contract

Later that evening, I sit on my bed and take a second look at Christopher's sex contract; I'm still bemused and I really can't tell whether he is trying to be funny or offensive. Surely the whole point of this is so that we can engage in some down and dirty kinky sex, yet there is nothing remotely sexy about a contract. In fact as I take it out of the brown envelope, my inner goddess thinks I'm reading a job specification or mortgage application; she has put her hair in a neat bun, and is wearing her librarian style suit complete with black rimmed spectacles, in an effort to make herself look intelligent and sensible.

It has also occurred to me that this contract is twenty pages long, twenty pages! This geezer clearly has far too much time on his hands and it is a wonder how he keeps his multi-million pound company running. Come to think of it, other than the odd phone call I don't think I have ever seen him do a stroke of work. He is far too busy playing the piano, eating, riding in helicopters and having sex. Well I guess I might as well take a proper look at this contract, just for shits and giggles...

The following terms form a binding contract between the Dominant and the Submissive.

Well this part certainly made me laugh out loud- the sheer irony; binding contract...

Both parties agree that everything under the terms of this contract will be consensual, confidential, and subject to the safety procedures set out in this contract.

Confidential- well I certainly won't be shouting from the rooftops that this bloke intends to tie me up and slap me, my mother would have a fit and as for safety procedures; it makes it sound as though he will do a risk assessment of my vagina, making sure that my work area is kept clean, safety goggles are worn at all times and spilled liquid, oil or grease are cleaned up immediately.

Neither party should suffer from sexual, serious, infectious or life-threatening illnesses including but not limited to HIV, Herpes and Hepatitis.

Does that include a cold and the flu as well? There is nothing worse than kissing someone with snot breath, especially when they've got all that crusty red skin around their nostrils from blowing their nose too much.

Miss Stevens will make herself available to Mr Green from Friday evenings through to Sunday afternoons each week.

Friday to Sunday; he's got to be having a laugh! I am a very busy woman at the weekends; Friday night Eastenders followed by a couple of Bacardi Breezers and WKDs in the local pub. Saturday morning, nurse hangover. Saturday afternoon, Home & Away omnibus. Saturday night, X Factor then TOWIE. You forgot Midsomer Murders and Antiques Roadshow. Shhh, that's supposed to be our secret; I don't want people to think I'm sixty five.

The Dominant will pay for any travel costs incurred by the Submissive.

Well I should bloody hope so, I've got about five quid left on my Oyster card and I hear the train fares are going up yet again in January. And if he thinks I'm riding a Boris Bike, he's got another thing coming- there is nothing worse than sweaty saddle crotch.

The Dominant must maintain his own good health and seek medical attention if necessary in order to maintain a risk-free environment.

Hmmm this geezer likes to inflict pain on women in his spare time, shouldn't he already be seeking medical attention? My inner goddess applauds my subconscious' comment.

The Dominant must not lend his Submissive to another Dominant.

Jesus, are there are whole groups of Christopher Greens out there who pass women around like Pokemon cards?

The Submissive must ensure that she obtains oral contraception and ensure that she takes it as and when prescribed to prevent any pregnancy.

Oral contraception? I'm presuming he's talking about the pill... Now Kayleigh has told me about this; I like the possibility of getting bigger tits, but a bigger arse and hips- not so much.

The Submissive will agree to any sexual activity asked for by the Dominant and shall do so without hesitation or argument.

Well I can't really say I'm too happy about this; what if it's a duvet day and I just want to wear my Primark tracksuit bottoms, eat a family sized bag of Kettle chips (all in one go you greedy cow, reminds my subconscious) bleach my moustache and watch Come Dine With Me?

The Submissive must not look directly into the eyes of the Dominant except when she is instructed to do so. The Submissive must keep her eyes cast down and maintain a quiet and respectful attitude in the presence of the Dominant.

Not look into his eyes, what the hell is that all about? Maybe he's a bit cross-eyed and he doesn't want me to notice, or maybe he suffers from bouts of conjunctivitis and he doesn't want me to see all the gloopy eye-pus stuck to his eyelashes.

The Submissive must always conduct herself in a respectful manner towards the Dominant and can only address him as Sir, Mr. Green, or any other such title that the Dominant may choose.

Sir is just not sexy. I make a mental note of all the Sirs that I know of; Cliff Richard, Elton John, Terry Wogan, Bruce Forsythe, Paul McCartney... all about as sexy as a colonic. The last person I actually called Sir was Mr Helier my Geography teacher; he wore brown, corduroy, ankle swinger trousers and his belly was so big that it could be seen hanging out of the bottom of his shirt, all pasty white doughy skin, with his navel pubis line spouting angry looking, coarse wiry hairs.

The Submissive must not take part in any activities or sexual acts that the Dominant feels may be unsafe.

Well I'm guessing that my favourite hobby of naked hang-gliding is out of the question then? You're not funny Annabella.

The safety word "Yellow" will be used to alert the Dominant that the Submissive is close to her limit of endurance.

Personally I would have chosen four safe words; "That hurts you fucker".

The safety word "Red" will be used to bring to alert the Dominant that the Submissive cannot tolerate any further demands.

A punch in the face would have a similar effect.

The Submissive will eat regularly (to maintain her health and wellbeing) from a prescribed list of foods. The Submissive must not snack between meals, with the exception of fruit and vegetables.

No snacking in between meals? Are you kidding me!! Well, unless the list of prescribed foods contains Kit Kat Chunkies, Crispy Crème doughnuts, MacDonald's hot fudge sundaes and extra hot Doritos, he can take his contract and jog on. Clearly you should be the one jogging Annabella, remarks my subconscious, your diet screams heart attack and saddlebag thighs.

The Dominant will provide the Submissive with a personal trainer four times a week for hour-long sessions. Times will be mutually agreed between the personal trainer and the Submissive.

The term 'personal trainer' conjures up horrid images of sweat bands, legwarmers, leotards and vests. The thought of bending and stretching for an hour, whilst my cheap leggings have given me camel toe, is the final straw for my inner goddess.

No acts involving fire play are allowed.

What on earth does he have in mind? He's already shown me a rather impressive burst, so surely there'd be no need for rockets or roman candles. Perhaps he wants to dance around naked waving sparklers- well that could be dangerous if you hold your sparkler too low down, I wonder if that's what the Kings of Leon meant when they said 'Your Sex is on fire'...

No acts involving urination or defecation (and the products thereof) are allowed.

My inner goddess has not only thrown up, she has also put on a chastity belt and biohazard suit. Clearly other people's shit and piss is not her thing.

No acts involving needles, knives, cutting, piercing, or blood are allowed.

I cry if I get a paper cut, faint when I give blood and had to get blind drunk to cope with having my ears pierced. This one is a no brainer.

No acts involving breath control are allowed.

Well, after getting a whiff of his morning breath yesterday, this might actually be a good thing.

My eyes skim across the text, to the part where it asks what sexual acts are acceptable to the submissive. After a list of some very dubious activities, I come across a line which says 'Is Bondage acceptable to the Submissive? Hands in front, hands behind back, ankles, knees, elbows, blah blah blah. I am very confused- are we supposed to be having sex or doing the Hokey Cokey?

My eyes start to droop and I am really becoming bored of reading the same repetitive waffle. This contract is never ending; dominant, submissive, intercourse, whipping, etc... etc... Time for a Kit Kat Chunky I think.

Chapter 11 - Sweaty Feet

Christopher has given me a MacBook Pro, well he says it is on loan, but it is quite obvious that it is mine to keep. Besides, if he knew me at all, he would know that it is not a good idea to lend me things for I never return them. When people lend me things, they either end up lost or ruined. There was the silk scarf that Kayleigh let me wear to a party; that ended up in the bin after I threw up all over it due to too many Sambuca shots (despite several washes, I couldn't get the stains or stench out- Sambuca with Thai Green Curry is not a good combination). Then there was the book that my mum lent me; pages 6, 7, 8 and 9 are now illegible after I spilt Ben and Jerry's cookie dough ice cream on them- not only are the words smudged but the whole book smells like gone off milk. My cousin's earrings are still in the 'safe place' I put them in and have yet to find.

I'm not really sure why he has given me this particular device; he knows I'm not a techno geek and it is a gesture which hardly screams romance or even sex (unless of course he is expecting me to use it to look at hardcore porn, which somehow I doubt). I would have much preferred a handbag, some shoes, perfume or even a box of Belgian chocolates. I am informed by the delivery guy that it will enable me to send emails and surf the net, whoopee fucking doo; it is 2013 not

1990 and I'm a university student in one of those big buildings that has electricity and computers and printers and, shock, horror, Wi-Fi. Yet obviously Christopher thinks I've been living in some remote jungle in Papua New Guinea.

I turn the laptop on to discover that I have an email from Christopher, my heart leaps into my mouth- I have an email from Christopher Green! Seriously Annabella, how long are you gonna keep this up for, wails my subconscious, are you really going to make a big deal out of every little thing he does...? 'Christopher Green is in my room', 'I'm in the bath with Christopher Green', 'I'm in Christopher Green's bed', 'Christopher Green is taking a shit'. Get over it will you, you've had his cock up your minge, so I really don't see why you're getting so excited over a flippin' email from him. And please will you stop calling him by his full name all the time, he is not a superior being- he is a woman beater and let's face it Annabella, no matter how much you tell yourself he has copper highlights, he's a GINGER!

Ignoring my subconscious (who really needs a nice Chamomile tea to help her chill out), I type a reply to Christopher's email. He replies in a nanosecond. Once again I reply, and yet again he replies at lightning speed. So he really has nothing better to do than send emails back and forth all day. The word 'loser' springs to mind. I could bore you with the contents of our emails for the next nine pages, but the student union bar is selling Vodka Jellies for a quid tonight, so I need to get a wriggle on. So, to summarise, it goes something along the lines of this...

"Have you had a good day at work?"

"Yes thanks, have you?"

"Yes thanks"

"Now stop emailing and do some work"

"No you stop emailing"

"No you first"

Blah di blah, you get the gist; an extremely loud, arms outstretched, not even bothering to cover your mouth yawn. Even my usually gobby subconscious has developed narcolepsy.

I decide to go for a run, not because I enjoy exercise (perish the thought), but because I saw Kayleigh in a pair of skimpy shorts this morning; the sight of her smooth, toned legs made me want to shove chocolate éclairs down her throat until she could no longer breathe. Whilst I stared at her in envy, my inner goddess was getting to work on making a little Kayleigh voodoo doll.

Fifty Hues of Hairy Legs and Morning Breath

I run for about five minutes and when I return my hair is stuck to my face, which incidentally is the colour of a radish and I feel as though I am about to hyperventilate. I can barely get to the end of the road these days without feeling like I am about to collapse; I really need to ditch the Kit Kats and Bacardi Breezers. Just as I am about to reach down and take my trainers off (£10.99 from Matalan) I sense someone behind me. I spin around and Christopher is standing in the doorway of my bedroom, behind him I see Kayleigh looking at me apologetically. I have a vision of grabbing her by the neck and smashing her head against the wall until her skull caves in, whilst cutting off her fingers one by one. She has known me long enough to understand how much I hate people turning up without ringing first. It all started when Juan turned up at our flat unannounced, I had literally bumped into him in the living room with a slither of Imac across my top lip.

"But he's your friend," Kayleigh had tried to reason. "It's not as if you fancy him."

"I don't give a shit whether it is my friend or the bloke from the Chinese Takeaway, I do not want anyone to know that until the Imac comes out I look like Groucho Marx!" I had hissed. Since then I have insisted that no one, with the exception of my mother, is to visit me without calling first.

"Good evening Annabella," says Christopher. Good, there is really nothing good about this evening; my hair is frizzy, my eyes are all bloodshot and piggy looking and I'm wearing my saggy around the arse and knees tracksuit bottoms and homeless person fading hoodie. I wonder whether I can pretend I haven't seen him; I could close my eyes like little kids do when they're playing hide and seek. Or perhaps I could say I'm Annabella's twin sister, we were separated at birth and I speak very little English. Maybe I could suddenly fall on the floor and pretend to be dead!

"H…h…h… hi Christopher," I stammer. Bollocks, he's seen me.

"Annabella, I felt that your email warranted a reply in person."

Oh did you really, and I suppose it would have been far too difficult to pick up the phone and call first? I can feel the rage building up inside me.

"I wondered what your bedroom would look like," he says.

I quickly scan the room checking that there are no dirty knickers or greying bras tossed on the floor. Shit! I can see a chicken fillet. I wait until he is not looking and kick the offending item under the bed.

He sits down on my bed and I sit beside him, he reaches over and undoes one of my pigtails. Well I wasn't going to say anything but since we're on the subject, pigtails should only be worn by girls under the age of ten, thirty-five year old porn stars who are trying to look like school girls, or German ladies at beer festivals. They do not make you look cute, or sexy- they make you look like a twat. My subconscious can be so rude at times. Christian seems to like them, so I don't really care what she thinks. Yes but Christian also likes to slap women and stick things up their bum, plus he never seems to brush his hair and he's ginger, so he's hardly an expert.

Christopher leans closer towards me. Oh God, please don't tell me he wants sex now. Surely he can see I've just been for a run. I'm sweating from every pore, and any moisture in between my legs certainly isn't from being aroused. Can't he wait until I've had a bloody shower? Suddenly he is lying on top of me and is kissing me, his tongue moving around inside my mouth. Gross, I bet I've even got sweaty breath. He slides off me and kneels down by my feet then he starts to undo one of my trainers. I try to push him off but as he has fastened me to the bed with his tie, my attempts are futile.

"Don't!" I protest as he undoes the laces. "I've just been running, I'm all sweaty."

He ignores me and pulls my trainer off, not only do my feet stink but I have a hole in my sock and my big toenail, which I have not had time to trim, is poking through. My inner goddess has begun to retch loudly whilst searching for some air freshener and Odour Eaters. Christopher pulls my sock off and as he does so, I notice that the cheap material has left black fluff in between each of my toes and under my toenails; it makes it look as though I haven't washed my feet in days. He seems unfazed by this and slowly begins to remove my tracksuit bottoms, it is then that I remember I am wearing my Bridget Jones style comfy knickers! They are hideous, a sort of gone-off flesh colour, and they are so big a family of Native Americans could use them to cover their wigwam. Christopher begins to remove his clothes. I stare at his six pack, defined pecs and tight buttocks, and my subconscious begins to make the calculations. Right, he's twenty seven now, so I give him roughly fifteen more years until the love handles, moobs and wrinkly arse cheeks start to make an appearance.

"I think you've seen enough," he suddenly says and he pulls my T-shirt up over my face, it is all bunched up over my eyes so that I cannot see a thing. I'm a little bit scared of the dark so to be honest this really isn't doing it for me.

"I'm going to get a drink," he informs me.

What? He's tied me up and blindfolded me and now he's off to the pub? I don't think so matey.

"Relax," he says, clearly sensing that I'm rather pissed off "I'm going to the kitchen."

Little bit rude I think. Not really sure I'm happy with him helping himself to whatever's in my fridge, which let's be honest, as I'm a student isn't really going to be a great deal. Apparently though, I don't just have cupboards full of baked beans (Lidl of course, not Heinz) and Pot Noodle, or a fridge full of cheap cider and dubious looking left over pasta, I am a student who can constantly afford to have white wine- and not just cheapo screw top wine at that, for I hear a cork popping followed by ice plinking at the bottom of a glass. I also hear voices and I know that he is talking to Kayleigh in the kitchen; she'd better not be eyeing up his pecs and six pack, the bitch.

Christopher returns to the bedroom and I can hear him removing his trousers. I hope he is going to pick all of his clothes up from the floor when he's finished, I really don't have time to be tidying up after him. He sits astride me.

"Are you thirsty?"

I am actually and come to think of it I'm a bit peckish too, a cheese and pickle sandwich would go down a treat right now, I wonder if he'll make me one.

"Yeah," I reply and before I know it he is kissing me, pouring the wine into my mouth as he does so. I have to resist the urge to spit it out; I have always been taught not to share knives, forks, toothbrushes, lollipops or anything else that has been in another person's mouth. 'You're just opening yourself up to a whole host of germs Annabella,' my mother had warned. Christopher leans towards me again and this time he deposits a small pool of ice and wine into my belly button. I feel the liquid overflow out of my navel and I immediately tense my body. I only changed my bed sheets this morning and I swear to God if any of that bloody wine goes on them I will have to punch him. Anyway, to cut a long and rather boring story short, we end up having sex and obviously I end up having about fifteen orgasms- because that wouldn't be unrealistic at all would it? In fact the way I'm going, he could stick it in my ear and I'd be having multiples.

Chapter 12 – Dinner

I have a date with Christopher, I think he wants to discuss the sex contract. I am getting ready and it is not going well; my GHD's decided to blow up half way through trying to tame my frizz, I managed to cut my legs twice while shaving and I have bugger all to wear. I want to appear sexy, yet elegant. I have thrown numerous garments across the room because they do not fit the look I am trying to achieve; animal print vest top-too Kat Slater, short turquoise dress- too TOWIE, pin-striped waistcoat- too Ellen DeGeneres, pale yellow tailored skirt and matching jacket- yeah, why don't you throw in a hat and some pearls too, I hear the 'Her Majesty' look is really sexy these days. This is just no good, my bedroom floor looks like sale time at Primark. After rummaging through my wardrobe and the floor another five times, I eventually decide on a black shift dress and high heels.

By the time I reach my car, which is parked miles away (I do have to remind myself though that, as a student in London, I'm lucky that I can afford to run a car and eat) I realise that the high heels are a big mistake; the balls of my feet are throbbing and I can feel a blister developing on the little toe of my right foot. The pain is making me hobble in a bizarre fashion that is a cross between Mick Jagger and a baby deer that has just learnt to walk.

I arrive at the hotel where Christopher is staying and walk into the bar. He is standing there sipping a glass of wine. He is wearing a white linen shirt, black jeans, black tie and a black jacket. My subconscious is having a field day. Well I can see we're going to have to sort out his dress sense, she exclaims, Jeans with a tie; what was he thinking? It's like wearing a suit with trainers, or shorts with loafers, or a waistcoat with a T-shirt. In fact, it is almost as bad as wearing white socks with black shoes! It's just wrong. I also notice that once again, he has not bothered to brush his hair.

"What would you like to drink? They have an excellent wine cellar here."

To be honest I really couldn't care less about their wine cellar. I'm certainly no wine snob. I remember going to a winery with my mum and hearing all the wannabe connoisseurs saying things like 'Hmmm I'm getting the subtle tones of chocolate and roast beef', or 'I can taste a faint hint of walnut and coffee', and I remember thinking oh please, it tastes of grape for fuck sake. I really don't see the point of paying twenty quid for a bottle of wine that's just going to be urinated out anyway. And to be quite honest, I think it's bloody disgusting that people squander hundreds of pounds on wine and champagne, when there are children all over the world who don't even have access to clean drinking water, Calm down Bob

Geldof, says my subconscious, raising her eyebrows. I'm not sure whether I'm in the mood for alcohol anyway, I'm thirsty and fancy something nice and refreshing. A tropical Um Bongo perhaps, or a can of Tizer (you can tell it's Tizer when your eyes are shut you know, not like Christopher's poncey wine). I take a look at my surroundings- not really the fizzy pop kind of place. You'll be expecting a vending machine selling Cheesy Wotsits and Lenny Henry to pop up next, tuts my subconscious.

"Are you hungry?" Christopher asks, once he has ordered me a glass of wine of his choice.

Come to think of it, I am. I wonder where he's going to take me; I could murder a Double Whopper with Cheese. Ooh, maybe we could go to Nando's, I just need one more stamp on my loyalty card to get a free quarter chicken and fino side. Don't be ridiculous Annabella, scolds my subconscious, he's a millionaire, he's not going to take you to bloody Nando's. She's right, it's bound to be somewhere far more upmarket; Pizza Express maybe?

"We can eat here- or in my suite?" Christopher asks. My heart sinks a little bit; Pizza Express do great dough balls.

"I don't mind."

"Come then."

He holds out his hand. "I have a private dining room booked." Not really sure why he bothered asking me then.

I take his hand and he leads me out of the bar, up the stairs and onto the mezzanine floor where a man directs us through to an intimate dining room with one secluded table. Blimey, this is a bit posh. I probably shouldn't ask for ketchup and mayo with my dinner.

"I've ordered already," he says as we take our seat. "I hope you don't mind." Well actually I flaming well do, who the hell does he think he is? I have a whole list of preferences and culinary do's and don'ts. I hope he hasn't ordered anything green (don't want to have spinach teeth) or spaghetti (too splashy) or any kind of pulses (gives me terrible wind) or fish (nothing worse than when they serve it with the head on and the goggle eyes stare at you) or anything with Parmesan (stinks like old men's feet). And if he's ordered anything that's going to give me garlic, onion or curry breath, then I'll be chucking it in the nearest pot plant.

"I hope you like oysters."

I have never had them but I've heard they taste like snot. I also know that they're an aphrodisiac, so I'm presuming he's trying to get me into bed again- would've been much cheaper just to get me pissed on a couple of bottles of cider, but hey ho. The oysters arrive at our table; they look like giant bogeys in shells.

Fifty Hues of Hairy Legs and Morning Breath

Not really sure how something resembling a bogey can be an aphrodisiac, but I watch as Christopher squirts some lemon juice onto one and tips it into his mouth. Great, not only does it look gross shovelling food into his mouth like Jabba the Hutt, but he'll have fishy breath too. My inner goddess has given up already and has gone to pluck the hairs on her chin and watch a bit of Corrie.

"Delicious," he says. "Tastes like the sea." Well that's not really making me want to try one. The last time I tasted the sea was when I nearly drowned in Corfu because I hadn't put my snorkel on properly; Stavros, the bloke who put out the sunbeds and umbrellas, had to swim out to get me. I was mortified when I discovered that not only was I only about five metres away from shore, but that during my thrashing around trying not to die, my bikini bottoms had come undone and the whole beach was getting an eyeful of my beef curtains.

"Go on Annabella, try one," he urges. "It's lovely, just put into your mouth all in one go." I bet he says that to all the ladies. I pick one up, eyeing it suspiciously. Christopher is watching me intently; I don't like people watching me eat at the best of times, but especially not when I'm about to put a giant bogey in my gob. I take a deep breath then tip the oyster into my mouth.

"Well, how is it?"

"Lovely," I lie, not wanting to seem unsophisticated. It's rank; it tastes like salty phlegm and I have to try very hard not to gag.

Once we have finished our starter, we begin to discuss the contract and his proposal to make me his submissive. Clearly I have had a lobotomy during my sleep, because I am slowly coming round to the idea. But while my inner goddess has already rushed out to buy her gimp suit, my subconscious is far from happy and in between the expletives and calling me a moron, she burns her bra, dons a pair of dungarees and begins reading a copy of The Female Eunuch.

Very soon our main course is at the table. Black cod (eurgh, what the fuck is that?) asparagus (if he thinks I'm giving him a blow job tonight he can think again- if it makes wee stink, God only knows what'll do to his sperm) and crushed potatoes with Hollandaise sauce (personally I would have preferred chips with a bit of Heinz mayonnaise and I have the urge to tell the waiter that someone appears to have sat on my potatoes). Only a few minutes later, I place my knife and fork neatly down on my plate. Christopher looks at me in shock.

"You've hardly eaten anything!"

"I've had enough."

"A couple of oysters, a few bites of your fish and an asparagus stalk is hardly a meal Annabella."

Blimey what is he, the food police? I haven't the heart to tell him that the reason I can't finish this probably very expensive dinner is that, throughout the course of the day, I've munched on a family sized bag of peanut M&Ms, three Findus Crispy Pancakes and a couple of Bird's Eye Potato Waffles, all washed down with diet Irn-Bru. Well come on, I don't wanna get fat do I?

Chapter 13 - Graduation

Today is the day of my graduation ceremony and would you believe who will be handing out the degree certificates- yep Christopher Green. Oh my God, will you please stop using his full name, I think they know who Christopher is by now, we're on chapter thirteen you moron!

I'm rather nervous about seeing him especially as our last meeting didn't end too well. Firstly, he doesn't like my car and thinks it is not road worthy, so he wants to buy me a new one which I really don't feel comfortable about. You idiot! You're a student, you're going to be knee deep in debt, you don't have a job yet and your car is a heap of shit; a millionaire is offering to buy you a car and you're saying no- are you insane? Most women your age are lucky to get a bottle of Bulmer's pear cider, half a bag of chips and a train ride home from their fuck buddies. The really lucky ones might also get a bout of Gonorrhoea or genital warts too! I'm not insane, I'm just not as mercenary as my subconscious. Secondly, I'm still not sure whether I will sign his sex contract; I just don't think he'll ever be able to commit properly and offer me a normal relationship. No shit. You've only just worked this out now? Wow, you really are dumb. (My inner goddess however, is not quite as dismissive of the idea; she's already had a Vajazzle, has been tuning into

Babe Station to try and learn some new moves and has even purchased the entire summer collection from Anne Summers- right now she's munching her way through a bag of marshmallow willies). Finally, he is going to see me in my graduation gown, which is about as sexy as a Monk's Habit.

I stare in the mirror and am appalled by how horrific I look in my gown; the length is most unflattering, making my ankles look fat, and the wide shapeless arms make me look as though I am wearing Dracula's cape. As for the hat, not only is it going to give me really bad hat hair, but it is far too big and keeps slipping over my eyes. Sighing in despair, I put on some dangly earrings to try and glam the whole outfit up a bit, but one glance at my reflection tells me they are far too Pat Butcher. I look like Uncle Fester in drag.

Kayleigh has already left as she is giving a speech during the ceremony (I bet she'll still manage to look gorgeous in her gown- the bitch) so I'm in the flat alone waiting for Ralph. I call Ralph my dad, except that he's not; he's kind of my stepdad, even though he's not with my mum anymore as she's remarried, basically my real dad is dead and my mum's been round the block a bit, it's all rather Jerry Springer. When Ralph arrives, he is wearing an ill-fitting beige suit with a black shirt and black tie; he would look like a pimp were it not for the fact that the trousers are ankle swingers and he has his flasher rain mac on over the top of it. Great, a cross between a pimp and a paedophile, it's going to be a long day. Oh well, at least we'll look like shit together.

We arrive at the auditorium and take our seats, me with the other graduates and Ralph with the other proud (and soon to be bored shitless) parents and guests. It dawns on me that as my last name is Stevens, I will have to wait bloody ages to collect my certificate. This is going to be extremely long and dull. I'm going to have to clap and pretend to be pleased for a bunch of people I don't even know, my hands are going to get sore, I'll probably need to pee half way through and I can't even play Tetris as I've had to switch my mobile off. I wonder if anyone will notice if I have a little nap. Should've just opted to have my certificate posted. To top it all off, I am sitting in between two highly irritating girls who feel the need to have a conversation across me.

"Oh my days, is that that millionaire bloke Christopher Green?"

"He's well fit ain't he!"

"Yeah he's buff, has he got a girlfriend?"

"Nah, someone told me he's gay!"

I turn to one of them and smile sweetly "He's not, he likes muff diving." That shuts them up.

The ceremony is just as boring as I thought it would be. I sit and watch Professor Copely pick his nose, really rooting around with his index finger as though he's searching for treasure, and Professor Adams, fallen asleep with his mouth open, little pools of drool clinging to the hairs of his bushy grey beard. Finally my name is called and I begin to rise from my seat in my horrible Addams Family outfit. I pray that I don't trip as I walk up the steps or worse, fall over on stage. I'm also rather worried that I'll need to pass wind just as I'm smiling for the photographer; double bacon, eggs and beans for breakfast was not such a good idea. Once again I also wish I was invisible as I really don't want Christopher to see me looking this hideous. Perhaps I could pull my hat right over my face so he doesn't recognise me, maybe pull all my hair over my face like Cousin It and just tell people afterwards that I thought we had to come in fancy dress.

I arrive on the stage and Christopher hands me my certificate, I shake his hand like every other graduate has done. It's sweaty. Really sweaty. My inner goddess coughs up a bit of bile. He asks me why I've been ignoring his emails; I tell him that I haven't checked my phone or laptop this morning. I want to tell him that his hands feel clammier than a sumo wrestler's crevices and that I'm worried about the germs multiplying on them after having shook the hands of over three hundred people. I hope he has anti-bacterial hand sanitiser. My inner goddess starts to cry; she's a little mysophobic and the thought of Staphylococcus and Streptococcus anywhere near her, are not the kind of cockus she was hoping for today.

After all the degrees have been handed out, we make our way out of the auditorium and through to the foyer where there are drinks and snacks- well, some shit booze and limp sandwiches, it's not Oxford or Cambridge. I find Ralph and we get a drink. Cheap fizzy wine, Christopher will not be impressed, I think it's bloody delicious though and wonder whether I can nick a bottle; I bet no one will notice if I shove it under my cape. Such a classy bird. I spy Kayleigh in the distance and turn to Ralph.

"I won't be a second, just need to speak to Kayleigh."

I head over to her to tell her how great her speech was, hoping she doesn't ask me which bit I liked best as I wasn't actually listening; I was far too busy watching Professor Noonan fiddling with himself in the back row. Dirty bastard.

"Christopher wants to speak to you," Kayleigh whispers when I reach her.

I look behind her and see him walking along with one of the professors, he catches my eye and shakes hand with the professor (not professor Noonan and his willy fingers thankfully) before saying goodbye. He strides over to me, looks around shiftily then suddenly drags me into a disabled toilet, locking the door behind him. What, he can't seriously want sex now, here? The loo stinks of stale wee and there is a dubious looking stain on the back of the door. Someone has scrawled 'call this number for blowjobs' on one of the walls. I look at the digits underneath; I swear that's Kayleigh's mobile number. Further down someone has also written 'Annabella is a Vergin' in black felt tip, I'm more angry with the fact that someone in this campus can't spell rather than the fact that people are making comments about my private life. Aside from the fact that there are a whole host of potential lurgies festering in the cubicle, it is also quite clear that this gown certainly wasn't designed for a quickie. By the time I've lifted up all the layers of material and pulled down my tights, his penis will barely be a semi and I'm not sure I've got the energy to wake it up again.

"I can't leave Ralph for too long," I tell him.

"Ralph's here, why didn't you say? I'd love to meet him."

Bollocks, I'm really not in the mood for the whole father-boyfriend introduction thingy. He's not your boyfriend, he's your potential Dominant, hah good luck explaining that one! She has a point. What will I say to Ralph? 'Ralph this is Christopher, he's not my boyfriend because he's got issues, but we're fucking like dogs on heat. He wants to whip, cane and beat me while I'm hog tied and then he'd like to stick things up my bum. Oh whoops, but he doesn't want me to tell anyone so

I've signed an NDA'. Hmmm, I can't imagine that Ralph's response will be anything like, 'Oh Annabella I'm so pleased for you, there's nothing like a man who knows want he wants. Perhaps we can go fishing together and he can tell me all about anal fisting, it'll be swell.'

We both walk back over to where Ralph is standing and I see that Kayleigh and her brother are walking towards him too. They reach him first and just as we get there, I hear Kayleigh say to Ralph, "So have you met Annabella's boyfriend yet?"

Stupid, stupid big-mouth snitch.

"Ralph, this is Christopher my boyfriend, Christopher, this is Ralph my father."

"It's a pleasure to meet you Ralph," says Christopher, holding his hand out to Ralph.

"Likewise." I can almost hear Ralph's thoughts- 'Hurt my baby girl and I'll cut your testicles off and make you eat them. Just for the record though, I know you're rich so you'll be paying for the wedding, I've got fuck all money'.

Ralph excuses himself to go to the toilet and while he's away, Christopher asks me about the contract. I don't know whether it's all the sexy professors with their corduroy jackets and elbow pads, the erotic speeches about alumni, the sight of Mr Clarke the librarian picking his nose and eating it, or the slightly stale ham sandwiches and garibaldi biscuits that have been provided for us, but I find myself agreeing to the terms of the contract and becoming his submissive. You fucking idiot! screams my subconscious. My inner goddess on the other hand has donned a Madonna style cone bra, thigh high PVC boots, a red leather mini skirt so short that her fanny is practically hanging out of the bottom and she's writhing around to Pussy Cat Dolls' 'Don't Cha'.

Later on Christopher comes over to celebrate my degree and to discuss the finer details of the contract.

"Ok Annabella, I'll agree to the no fisting, but I'd really like to take you up the bum, although your arse will need training first of course."

What? Arse training? WTF? Is he going to send my arse on one of those boring courses in the city where you have to listen to dull presentations and engage in stupid team building activities, then when the course leader says at the end 'does anyone have any questions?' there is always one eager beaver creepy crawly bum lick who has about ten. Or does he mean weight training, is he saying I've got a fat arse? Perhaps my arse is going to start an apprenticeship; carpentry, electrician, engineering? My subconscious for once says nothing, I think she has actually given up on me. My inner goddess is really flummoxed, she is looking at her behind in the mirror, poking and prodding her butt cheeks whilst doing her 'does my bum look big in this' face.

"Okay, so what about sex toys?" Christopher asks, pointing to the copy of the contract that he has brought with him. I glance at the list again to refresh my memory. Vibrators; does he mean like my Oral B electric toothbrush? That vibrates, surely the bristles would hurt my fanny though? Didos? I don't understand, how does he know Dido? I know he's a millionaire and all but I didn't realise he had connections with the music industry. I don't really see how she's a sex toy though, does he want me to have sex with her, can't really say she's my cup of tea, aside from the fact that I'm not a lesbian, I prefer brunettes and she might sing White Flag afterwards- so boring. I look at the list again, oh it must be a typing error- he means lilos. Oooh are we going to the beach, I love the beach! We're going to have sex on a lilo, how exciting. I hope we don't go too far out though, I'm not a very good swimmer, what if a shark comes along, or there are sea urchins?

Oh. My. God. How the hell did you manage to graduate? Can't you read, it says DILDO you stupid girl. It is something, usually penis shaped, that you put in your 'sex' as you like to call it. Oh, now I get it. Other vaginal/anal toys; how many can there be? Is there some kind of kinky Toys R Us, or X-rated Hamleys that I don't know about where they sell Lego men with huge penises and

Fifty Hues of Hairy Legs and Morning Breath

Lego women with double D breasts, Saucy Stickle Bricks and Erotic Etch a Sketch? If I pop into WHSmiths will I find Karma Sutra Kerplunk, Randy Rubik's Cube, Horny Hungry Hippos, Gloryhole Guess Who and Sluts & Ladders? I don't think I remember looking in the Argos catalogue and finding Bondage Barbie, Cunnilingus Care bears, My Little Penis, Anal Action Man, Felching Furby, Prostitute Peppa Pig or Bagpussy...

After I agree to everything outlined in the bondage part of the contract, we move onto the section about restraining. Genital clamps? Jesus, I hope he doesn't mean those big yellow ones that they use on your car. Suspension? I was suspended from school once for pulling Lucy Woodman's chair out from underneath her because she called my mum a smelly troll. Don't really see how that's sexy, what's he gonna do, suspend me from work or my flat? Next we move onto punishment, most of the methods are quite obvious but there are a few I don't get, paddling for example; does he mean in a pool or the sea? Neither is particularly arousing, I got frost bite once when I went paddling in the sea at Brighton. Nipple clamps? Again I pray that he doesn't mean the yellow car ones, I'm already worrying about my tits sagging with age.

Finally we come to the end of the contract, we've been drinking wine throughout and I'm starting to feel a bit tipsy, I should probably stop- the last time I was drunk near Christopher it did not end well. My inner goddess shudders as she remembers me throwing up into the azaleas, bits of regurgitated carrot stuck in my hair (why is there always carrot in vomit?). Christopher has put his wine glass down and looks at me with a serious expression.

"Before I take you to bed, there is just one more thing we need to talk about."

He takes my hand and lifts me off the sofa.

"Come, I'd like to give you your graduation present." He leads me to the hallway, opens the front door and there parked in front of my flat is a red hatchback Audi. My first reaction is that I really would have preferred black, red is so tacky. But then anger kicks in, I told him not to buy me a car, how can I accept it when we've only known each other for a few weeks? Make the most of it sweet cheeks, he's all presents and great sex now but you mark my words, ten years down the line and it'll be a packet of chocolate hobnobs followed by a quick shag with the lights off, socks and vest on.

I can't stay angry at him for long though, and the next thing I know we're in my bedroom and he is hitching my skirt up around my waist (don't worry, I shed the Uncle Fester graduation gown a while earlier). Suddenly his fingers rip through the material of my knickers. Blood rushes to my head and I feel my heart thumping; not because I'm so unbelievably turned on and can't wait to have him inside me, but because he has ripped my favourite La Senza knickers and I want to punch his face in! Well I bloody well hope he's gonna pay for a new pair, ripping underwear may be sexy in a Jilly Cooper novel, but I'm a jobless graduate, I can't afford to buy new knickers every time Mr Green wants to go all caveman on me. I think I would have preferred it if he'd said 'oi get yer knickers off treacle'.

Chapter 14 - Spanked

I'm about to get my first proper spanking since agreeing to be Christopher's submissive. He's angry because I rolled my eyes at him. Blimey it doesn't take much to make him angry, especially when I think of all the things that really deserve a slap:

1) Bald men with beards, I mean c'mon.

2) Baseball caps worn backwards or to the side, unless you're a rapper or under the age of ten.

3) Woman with humungous breasts who go topless (on the beach obviously, not doing their weekly shop in Tesco). We all need our vitamin D, but for some reason these women always feel the need to play bat and ball or Frisbee right by my sun lounger.

4) Kids in restaurants; I don't want to see little Emily blowing spit bubbles whilst I'm tucking into my seafood linguine; it's not cute and she's not adorable.

5) Middle class and Mediterranean men who wear jumpers (or sweaters as they would call them) around their shoulders or necks; it's not a shawl or a scarf it's a jumper, now put it on properly before I strangle you with it.

6) Fat men in vests; should be illegal especially if they have hairy shoulders...

I am brought back to reality by Christopher pulling my pyjama bottoms and knickers down. My inner goddess is nervous, she doesn't like pain; she has donned knee and shin pads, American Football shoulder pads plus safety goggles and a hard hat. My subconscious is incredulous; are you seriously going to let this man smack you, how humiliating! She's obviously forgotten that I am a white belt in karate and my wax-on wax-off technique is second to none. Christopher pulls my pyjama bottoms off completely and pulls me over his knee. I'm aware that my arse cheeks are on full view and hope that I'm not having a bad cellulite day. You had a Kit Kat Chunky and Nice N' Spicy flavour Nik Naks for breakfast, you do the maths.

He brings down the first blow on my bum cheeks, and I feel my arse wobble like a blancmange. Eighteen slaps later and he is finally finished, although I swear it takes another five minutes for my arse to stop juddering; I wonder if all that slapping will have knocked some of the fat out. When all the slapping is done, I wonder whether I should give him a taste of his own medicine. I could come over all Bruce Lee on him; get him in a headlock with my nunchucks then show him my best dragon pose. Maybe I could bust out a few of my wrestling moves; a drop kick followed by the John Cena spine buster. My inner goddess yawns, she's really not feeling in a Fist of Fury kind of mood.

Christopher is clearly in a shagging mood though, for he is now pulling my tracksuit bottoms off and moving me onto all fours. I hear the familiar sound of a condom being taken out of its wrapper and it suddenly occurs to me that I have never seen what he does with the condoms once he removes them, weird. Maybe he collects them and is making some strange sort of modern art style collage. Nothing would surprise me these days; on a recent visit to the Tate Modern I saw a piece where someone had simply stuck their bathroom cabinet to the wall, and another where it looked as though they had pulled out all of the fluff from their vacuum cleaner and stuck it on a wooden peg; these were both followed by poncey explanations about how they were deep and meaningful. It's probably more likely though, that the dirty sod is just shoving them all under my bed. I'll be able to open my own sperm bank soon, although I doubt there's much of a market for three week old crusty spunk.

Chapter 15 – Contraception

Christopher ended up staying over last night. Well rather he left and then came back; it's a long story which I won't bore you with, but maybe in the near future a movie could be made about it! Ian Somerhalder, Matt Bomer or Robert Pattinson could play Christopher, wouldn't that be awesome! Don't be ridiculous Annabella, Mick Hucknall would play him- they have the same hair.

Anyway, I found out that he's wanted to spank me ever since I asked him if he was gay during our interview. Is that a usual reaction to being asked if you're gay? Blimey, anyone interviewing Simon Cowell better watch out, I bet a slap from Mr Man Boobs, Bog Brush Hair would really smart. He also explained why he gets turned on when he hits me and that he needs to control me. This dude has some serious issues. I wonder whether we should go on the Jeremy Kyle show, although we'd probably have to put on a couple of pounds, forget to wash our hair and lose some teeth first.

There is a knock on the door, I open it and a man is standing there with a package. Before my inner goddess has a chance to start touching herself, I tell her that it is not that kind of package. She is turning into a right slut these days. He is quite fit though and she licks her lips and gives him a wink. The package is from Christopher. I open it and inside is a BlackBerry, I'm a little disappointed- I would have much preferred an IPhone. Putting the phone in my pocket, I grab my coat and make my way to my last ever shift at Wilkinson; now that we've graduated Kayleigh and I are moving out of the flat and looking for full time jobs in the city.

When I arrive at work Robin, my manager, has gone to get a coffee; I seize the opportunity and dig into the pic n' mix before the brat children come in and get their dirty mitts on them. I put on my horrible red Wilko fleece and take my place at the tills next to Maureen who is flirting with a male customer, poor sod looks terrified. Gary is not in today, sick apparently, maybe he's having his coco pop removed. He's been replaced by Jill, who always looks as though she is about to die. My shift seems to drag on, and the only thing that makes it remotely interesting is watching Terry the security guard arrest a woman who is nicking stuff and putting it in her toddler's buggy, and the weekly visit from the drunk who comes in with his can of Special Brew and tells all the other customers that they are 'lyin old goats'.

When I get home I receive a visit from Tyler, the weird creepy guy who is always lurking around Christopher. He has come to take my car away so that he can sell it for me. It turns out that he has worked for Christopher for four years. I wonder if he knows about Christopher's sex room? Perhaps he knows about it, but isn't allowed to talk about it- a bit like Fight Club. As I hand him the car keys, I can't help but wonder whether he heard us having sex the other day, for all I know he could have been standing behind the door with a glass to his ear. I'm fairly convinced that I'm quite quiet- not much of a screamer. Christopher on the other hand sounds as though he has Tourettes when he climaxes.

Juan joins Kayleigh and me at the flat later for takeaway- Dominos pizza. We're all packed, ready to move out of the flat, so we have to sit cross legged on the floor. Juan's wearing skinny jeans and I can see the outline of his penis. When we finish eating Ellis turns up and he and Kayleigh disappear off to her room- to shag undoubtedly (at least he doesn't say 'laters baby' again- if he did I've have to punch him)- so Juan and I go to the bar for a drink. When I get back, I discover that I have five missed calls and an angry voicemail from Christopher, who is mad because I didn't call him straight after work and he is worried. However, when I call him back, he sounds like he couldn't give him a shit. I can't keep track of his mood swings; I reckon he is Bipolar, or on crack. Eventually his mood seems to soften, and I can sense over the phone that he is smiling.

"You hang up," I tell him, giggling.

"No you hang up."

"I don't want to."

"I don't want to either."

Fucking hang up or I will ram the phone up your rectum and you and your pervert Christopher won't need to do any 'arse training'. Blimey, who rattled her cage?

Christopher has decided that I need some contraception as he's fed up of using condoms. Can't say I'm too keen on them either with their horrible smell and texture, but at least they're keeping me safe. I'm sure he's had his willy in a lot of places and although he tells me he's healthy how can I be sure? I don't want to catch anything nasty. I've heard all about pubic lice and crabs and they sound gross. If you get pubic lice does the nit nurse come round and start rooting around in your knickers with her silver comb? When my little cousin caught nits my auntie had to shave all her hair off, I don't really fancy anyone doing a Britney Spears on my muff. And crabs? What's that all about, I don't like the sound of finding Christmas Island in between my legs.

I will be seeing Dr Grier at Christopher's apartment this afternoon. This is just another reminder of how rich this guy is, he is able to get a doctor to come to his house on a Sunday. At my surgery, you're lucky if you can get an appointment on a weekday three weeks in advance. First you have to go through the whole process of dealing with the receptionist, who talks to you as though you are a dog turd. I'm sure that GP receptionists are the same world over, and that being rude and full of self-importance are prerequisites for the job.

When you finally get in to see the doctor, he or she will generally tell you that you have a virus, regardless of your symptoms. The waiting room will be filled with people coughing their guts up, old ladies who have come in to collect their incontinence medication, fat bastards who still don't understand why their blood pressure and cholesterol are high and scabby little kids with snot caked around their noses. You're likely to end up leaving sicker than you were when you arrived.

Doctor Grier is middle aged and plump with coffee breath. We shake hands and Christopher disappears into the kitchen to leave us to it. She asks me a lot of rather nosey questions about my sex life, then takes my blood pressure and weight. Next she proceeds to run through the various birth control methods.

"Now, if you don't fancy anything too heavy at the moment but you want an alternative to plain old condoms, there is the Femidom."

She unwraps then begins to unfold what looks a transparent rubber sock, it's massive and there is no way that's going anywhere near my front bottom; I may as well stick a plastic Co-op bag up my fanny. My inner goddess thinks she's taking the piss, she's laughing hysterically and is busy going through the kitchen drawers to see if she can fashion her own make-shift contraception; she has some cling film, sticky tape, Blu-Tack and a sandwich bag at the ready.

"Um, I think I'd like to see some of the other options," I tell Dr Grier, trying not to show my disgust.

"Ok, well there's the IUD; once it's in place you don't need to think about it, and it's very effective. The downsides are that it can be painful putting it in, and it can make your periods heavier." Heavier periods, ooh that sounds like such fun! Thanks but no thanks. Eventually I decide on the mini pill and she writes me a prescription for a six month supply.

When I return to the kitchen, Christopher is sitting at the breakfast bar eating. He doesn't notice that I am there for a few minutes and his true eating habits are revealed. He is shovelling food into his mouth like it is going out of fashion, making wet gulping noises and smacking his lips together like a Bulldog. He has ketchup all around his mouth which incidentally he doesn't feel the need to close, so I get glimpses of half chewed food churning around in his cake hole. He suddenly realises I am here and closes his mouth to chew, but not in time to catch a bit of egg yolk that falls onto his bottom lip. At this moment he is more Cookie Monster than sex god. My inner goddess is most displeased, she is off to watch The

Weakest Link and it'll take a lot to prise her legs apart again. I'm on her side and decide to go and have a nap.

I'm woken from my nap by lips kissing my forehead. I growl and roll over onto my other side, burying my head under the pillow. It's starting to get dark and I wonder how it is possible to develop morning breath a) in the evening and b) after a short nap. I also seem to have sweated gallons during my sleep, which means I have matted hair and stinking pits. I do not want to get out of bed, and if he kisses me or tries to rouse me from my slumber again, I will be tempted to breathe on him with my dragon breath and singe his eyebrows.

"Annabella wake up, we have to leave in half an hour." Ha ha, half an hour, he'll be lucky cackles my subconscious, does he really think that's all the time you need to get ready? It'll take a good twenty minutes just to have a dump, pluck your monobrow and get a comb through your rats tails. Half an hour, that's the funniest thing I've ever heard! I panic, she's right. I haul myself out of bed, the crusty patch on my pillow not going unnoticed, great I've been dribbling in my sleep.

Today I'm meeting Christopher's parents, it'll be the first time seeing his mother when I don't have just-had-sex-hair and the first time I've ever met his father. I'd better get ready quick smart. I look around on the floor for my underwear, I find my bra but my knickers are nowhere to be seen. Then I remember that Christopher put them in his pocket when we were in his sex room this morning. I'm going to have to go commando when I meet his parents! My inner goddess is loving it, she feels like Katie Price on a bender. She thinks she's in some cheap porn flick where she gets it on with the pizza delivery guy. My subconscious however, does not feel quite so liberated. You'd better make sure you wear trousers or a very long skirt; you don't want to do a Lindsay Lohan and give your potential father-in-law an eyeful of your bearded clam.

When we arrive at their home, Dr Tresilian-Green is standing on the doorstop waiting for us, and standing next to her is a man who I presume is her husband. I wonder what reaction I would get if I were to lift my skirt up and shout out, "Whoo hoo, get a load of this!" The house looks rather posh, so I decide against it. His mother kisses me on both cheeks; clearly she thinks we're in France. His father holds his hand out to me and I shake it firmly. I hear a high pitched voice from inside the house.

"Are they here yet?"

A girl of about my age appears on the doorstep, she has long dark hair, big boobs and a tiny waist. I hate her immediately. My inner goddess looks her up and down appreciatively and wonders whether she may be bi-curious.

"Annabella, this is my sister Mina."

"Hi Mina, it's nice to meet you." And your breasts, mutters my subconscious, noticing how low cut her dress is.

Dinner with his parents is a very posh affair and rather different from the sort of food he'd get if I took him to my folks, where anything from alphabet spaghetti to Angel Delight could be on the menu. Instead we are tucking into tiny portions of dishes with names that I can't even pronounce.

After dinner, Christopher excuses the both of us and says that he wants to give me a tour. My inner goddess is taking out her Ann Summers' naughty nurse costume, as she knows that giving me a tour really means that he wants to take me somewhere and shag me. We end up having a quickie in the boathouse and nearly get caught by Mina, who has clearly come to be nosey. I hope she's not some weird pervert who likes to watch or listen to her brother having sex. Nothing would surprise me about this family.

Chapter 16 - The Time of The Month

I have decided to go and visit my mum, who has a timeshare in Tenerife with her current husband Bill. I need to have a break from Christopher and all the madness. Plus I think my subconscious could do with abstaining from sex for a while, quite frankly she is turning into a right old slapper- she needs a cold shower and a pair of dungarees.

Christopher, being the flash git that he is, has secretly upgraded my Easyjet ticket to a first class British Airways seat. Hurrah! For once I'm not going to complain. I hate travelling on planes because they have people on them. But no Easyjet means no orange stewards (the orange referring to the colour of their skin as well as their uniforms) no fidgeting toddlers kicking the back of my seat, no groups of lads wearing tacky T-shirts and sombreros off to Dave's stag-do and no being ripped off for the in-flight snacks; I mean c'mon on, eight quid for a snack pack! Thieving bastards. Instead of the hell that is Easyjet, I've got a fully reclining leather window seat and I'm handed a champagne cocktail by the air steward. I wonder how the common people in economy class are.

My mum and Bill are waiting at the airport when I arrive and it is so good to see them. As soon as I have unpacked we head down to the beach. Once I am comfortable on my sun lounger, I look up and down at the different people who have chosen to holiday in the Canary Islands. I spy a heavily tanned peroxide blonde; she keeps adjusting her bikini top to show off the breasts that she's clearly spent a lot of money on. Further down the beach, I can see an old man with fuzzy grey chest and back hair spreading right across his shoulders and up to the top of his neck. This is alarming enough, but then I look down and see that he is wearing speedos; I nearly choke on my strawberry Cornetto.

To the other side is Morbidly Obese Lady, I look at her cellulite riddled legs and wish I had sat next to her, she would have made my sausage thighs look positively waif like. Small children stare at her in horror and it is probably because they are scared she may eat them. I wonder why they make swimming costumes so big. Once Obese Lady has moved I can see Prune Woman; she is so brown she is practically purple and her skin has taken on the dry, wrinkly appearance of a pair of leather gloves. She rubs factor 2 Hawaiian Tropics sun oil into her skin and then takes her position on her towel where she will inevitably stay for the next eight hours; she is practically a walking melanoma.

Further down is a father helping his young child build a sandcastle; how sweet I think, until I notice that in actually fact he is doing very little to help build the sandcastle and instead is staring at the tits of a group of topless teenage girls nearby. Finally I glance at the geezers, it is hard to tell whether they are on a stag do or a football tour, but it is very easy to tell that they are English. They are all either bright red or pasty white, they are all drinking plastic cups of lager and they all have man boobs or paunches, plus one of them has run into the sea and is mooning at the rest of his mates, his spotty arse cheeks ruining the horizon.

The next day we move from the beach to the pool, Bill and my mum dive straight in but I am hesitant; there are a group of children playing on their lilos and inflatable boats and there is no doubt that one of them will have peed in it.

I check my phone for messages; there is a text from Christopher. 'How many of those sangrias are u going 2 drink?' What? How does he know I'm drinking sangrias? Fuck, is he here?

"Good afternoon Miss Steele."

I turn around and there he is. He looks gorgeous, although slightly sunburnt on his nose- that'll be the ginger in him.

"Christopher! What are you doing here?"

"I was missing you, so I caught a flight this morning."

Can't decide whether I'm flattered that he's flown three hours to see me, scared that he is stalking me, worried that he's just missing the sex and slapping rather than my actual company, or pissed off that he may cramp my style- I've seen some really fit Spanish waiters since I arrived.

Later I invite Christopher to have dinner with us. Bill is indifferent but my mum seems to love him, she's probably just pleased that her daughter won't be left on the shelf. After dinner I go back to Christopher's hotel suite, we make love and then fall asleep.

I wake up at 6am with a pounding headache, sore tits and a desperate need for chocolate. I get up to pee and when I look in the mirror I discover I have a humongous zit near my mouth. Gross. I could disguise it as a mole but it is more Grotbags than Cindy Crawford. I burst into tears. I open Christopher's mini bar, there is no fucking chocolate. I burst into tears again. I get back into bed but can't get comfortable due to my sore boobs which feel as though they weigh six stone each. I can hear Christopher breathing softly, it is highly irritating and I want to get the pillow and smother him to death. In case you haven't guessed I am due on my period. Christopher has woken up and is gazing at me.

"What?" I snap at him. "What are you staring at?"

"Good morning beautiful," he replies and reaches out to stroke my cheek. I push his hand away and roll onto my other side. I feel his hand slide across my hip and along my thigh. He has got to be kidding me, he can't seriously want sex now. My stomach is bloated and I look as though I am five months pregnant, my ankles are puffy and my hair is greasy. I don't want to have sex, I want to sit in my pyjamas all day and eat chocolate, chocolate and more chocolate. In fact just food in general would be good right now. Maybe I should eat him.

"Let's order some breakfast from room service."

"Oh Annabella, I'm not hungry, at least not for food," he replies and cups my breast. I have an urge to get him in a headlock and break his arm. My inner goddess is calling him every expletive known to mankind and is even making some new ones up.

He dials room service and orders a croissant and an orange juice, 'and the same for my guest' I hear him say. Enraged, I grab the phone from him and order a croissant, scrambled eggs, sausage, beans, bacon, mushrooms, fried bread and a pain au chocolate. He looks at me horrified.

"Wow Annabella, are you hungry?"

"No, I thought we'd have a food fight," I reply sarcastically.

We both get dressed and wait in silence for our breakfast to arrive. His face is getting on my nerves and I can still hear him breathing. He begins to drum his fingers on the coffee table next to the sofa in his suite. I sigh and tut loudly but he does not get the message. If he does not stop I will find some pliers and remove his fingers one by one. He continues to drum his fingers and they make a steady rhythm on the table.

"Oh for fuck sake Christopher, make a bit more noise why don't you, they can't quite hear you in Lanzarote."

Breakfast finally arrives; I eat all of mine and have a bite of his croissant. I suddenly burst into tears again and fling my arms around him.

"Oh I'm so happy you came to see me," I blubber though half a ton of snot.

He looks at me, terrified. No doubt he is wondering where Annabella is and who this bizarre split personality, emotional wreck with the huge appetite is.

I go into the bathroom and run a bath. I stare down at my naked body; it is in desperate need of attention. Despite having had a leg and bikini wax before I flew out here, I have black hairs starting to poke their way through the skin on my shins. My bikini line is equally unattractive and has taken on the appearance of a plucked chicken, with a few ingrown hairs causing angry looking red bumps. I should either move to a country where it is considered sexy to be hairy, or I should start wearing a Burka.

After what seems like ten hours of plucking, shaving and scrubbing, I finally leave the bathroom. I have a shaving cut on the back of my ankle, the spot near my mouth seems to have doubled in size and my ankles resemble those of a sufferer of Elephantitis. This does not seem to put Christopher off however, for no sooner am I out of the bathroom than he has practically leapt on me and pulled my towel off. I don't feel remotely sexy and would sooner curl up in front of the telly with a nice box of chocolates. As he pushes me onto the bed and straddles me, I just hope he hurries up and gets on with it. The sooner it is over and done with, the sooner I can get to the vending machine and buy three Kit Kat Chunkies. Unless he wants to die, he'd better not even consider foreplay.

Chapter 17- Laters Baby

It is over between Christopher and me. I'm sure you're presuming that it is because of his controlling personality, the fact that he wants me to be his submissive rather than his girlfriend, the huge difference between our social and economic statuses, because it seems as though he is just using me for sex, or the fact that he has so many issues… well it is none of those. I have discovered something far, far worse about Christopher Green. I'd better explain.

Well, a lot has happened since Tenerife; Christopher and I have indulged in some more bondage, we have flown in his helicopter again and I have declared my love for him (I won't tell you how my subconscious reacted to this, but her potty mouth resembled that of a trucker).

Once I arrived home from visiting my mum, I unpacked and then decided to go and visit Christopher who had flown home a few days before me. I have really got a taste for this whole sex thing and I was even going to let him spank me again. I spent ages getting ready; de-fuzzing my bits, cutting my toenails and plucking the rogue hairs on my chin and I even put on the dress that always seems to get him horny.

When I arrived at his apartment, I was greeted at the door by Tyler. "Good evening Miss Stevens, I hope you had a pleasant flight home."

'Erm whateva creepy guy', is what I wanted to reply, but I didn't.

"Mr Green is in the shower right now, but I'm sure he'll have no objections to you waiting in his room."

It was all working out perfectly; I could go into his bedroom, remove my clothes and then surprise him by slipping into the shower with him. I was turned on just thinking about it and my inner goddess was practically wetting her knickers with excitement.

I got into his bedroom and began to remove my clothes, I could hear him singing the Macarena in the shower. I was just about to remove my bra when I noticed that his suitcase was on the floor, it was open and looked as though he was halfway through unpacking. I could see scrunched up socks, wrinkled shorts, damp swimming trunks and half empty toiletries. And then I made my discovery. My heart started to pound and I began to shake uncontrollably, tears streaming down my face. My inner goddess began to vomit violently, throwing up with such force until her body could take no more and she fainted, collapsing in a heap on the floor. I had laid eyes on something unforgiveable; for there in his suitcase, on a pair of his pants, were Christopher Green's skid marks...

Printed in Great Britain
by Amazon.co.uk, Ltd.,
Marston Gate.